International Incident

Melissa F. Miller
USA TODAY Bestselling Author

Brown Street Books

Copyright © 2016 Melissa F. Miller

Published by Brown Street Books.

For more information about the author,
please visit www.melissafmiller.com.

Brown Street Books ISBN: 978-1-940759-19-7

For Trevor

Acknowledgments

Many thanks to everyone involved in the production of this book, in particular, my phenomenal editing and design team. I would also be remiss if I didn't thank my husband and children. As I was writing this book, we reached a milestone: now every member of the family, from the youngest to the oldest, has the requisite skill set and motor control to deliver to Mom and her muse a much-needed cup of coffee. Thanks, kiddos.

If you have an opportunity to accomplish something that will make things better for someone coming behind you, and you don't do that, you are wasting your time on this earth.

—Roberto Clemente
(1934-1972)

1.

Tumpat, Malaysia

MINA LOWERED her head and kept her eyes fixed on the dusty ground, staring hard at a point just in front of her bare feet. She concentrated on not shaking.

This is it, she thought. *The last hurdle.*

She had cut her long, thick hair very short, cropping it close to her skull, and had stolen the neighbor boy's clothes from the line outside his hut just before leaving her village. The baggy shorts and thin, worn T-shirt hung on her frame. She just had to trust they obscured what curves she had. But still, she thought it best to blend into the crowd as much as possible, avoiding any close scrutiny.

The man from the manning agency barked his orders quickly, first in Malay and then again in Burmese, for the benefit of the somber men who huddled together off to the side, apart from the Malaysians. The instructions were deceptively simple. They were to line up to have their teeth and hands inspected. Then they would be separated into two groups: those who would be rejected and those who would have the good fortune to move on to staff fishing boats leaving from Songkhla, across the border in Thailand, in the coming days and weeks.

Before she shuffled into line, Mina took a long, centering breath. She had to get a spot on a boat. There was no money left. Her younger sisters' bellies were empty, and their father was too sick to work—closer now to joining her mother in death than to life. She had two options. The better of the two, by far, was to trick her way into a position on a male-only fishing crew, which the men in the village spoke of with open awe. The fishing crews made unimaginable sums, or so she'd heard.

If she was rejected from the crew, the other option was grim. She would have to make her way back to the village and grow her hair long again, then trade her tattered boys' clothing for a tight-fitting dress and heavy makeup and head for Kuala Lumpur to find work in "guest relations" at one of the clubs, satisfying the physical urges of tourists. A cold shiver of disgust ran along her spine and she stiffened as she fell into line behind the tall, talkative man from the bus.

She watched from under her eyelids as the agent for the labor company walked along the line. Most people were sent to the left to await the truck to take them to the port city in Thailand. A few were cast off to the right. Most were muttering softly, cursing their luck.

One old man, turned away—likely because he looked too frail to do the work—was weeping, begging, and waving bills. "I have the staffing fee. I have the fee," he shouted.

The agency man snapped his fingers and called the old man over. He fanned out the money and counted it, then nodded and jerked a thumb to the group to the left.

Mina hid a smile. She'd heard that most workers didn't have the staffing fee. This, in itself, was not a problem. The agency would front the money, and the crew member could work it off. But her father had given her his blessing to take what little money remained in the blue and white porcelain bowl that sat near his sleeping mat. She had the fee. She could buy her spot.

You can do this, she assured herself as she straightened her spine trying to project an air of vigor and strength. *You've got this.*

~ ~ ~ ~ ~ ~ ~ ~ ~ ~ ~

Port of Singapore, Cruise Centre

"You've got this," Connelly whispered in Sasha's ear, giving her hand an encouraging squeeze as they walked up the gangway track to board *The Water Lily.*

Sasha met her husband's concerned eyes and gave him a wobbly smile. "I know."

The rational part of her brain recognized that it was ludicrous to need a pep talk to embark on an eight-day, seven-night cruise through exotic locations in Southeast Asia, but rationality couldn't trump the reality: she missed her babies. And something behind Connelly's smile made her think he missed them just as much as she did. After all, the cruise hadn't been his idea, either.

The vacation had been a gift. A surprise arranged by Sasha's legal partners, purportedly because McCandless and Volmer, PC had just finished a phenomenal fiscal year. But Sasha knew Will Volmer well enough to know that his idea of a year-end bonus was a basket of fruit. *Maybe* a ham. Assuredly *not* a luxury cruise—and definitely not one that included international airfare for two, no less. No, the trip had Naya's fingerprints all over it—Naya had not only cleared Sasha's trial calendar, she'd arranged for Sasha's parents to babysit Finn and Fiona for the duration of the cruise. She herself was taking care of the cat and dog.

When Sasha had pointed out that Naya, as the firm's junior partner, had worked just as many hours as Sasha had, Naya and Will had countered that no one else had put up their billable hours while parenting newborn twins. Sasha suspected that the babies were only part of the reasoning behind the gift. She and Connelly had had a difficult year, to put it mildly. She thought he still needed to deal with the fallout from having found his father. In any case, her hesitation about being singled out had faded somewhat when Naya rolled into the firm's parking lot in a sparkling new Mercedes in place of her ancient Honda Civic.

As Sasha handed her cruise card to the broadly smiling crew member at the top of the ramp and waited for the woman's handheld scanner to beep, registering her card, she made a mental note to chat with Will about the firm's finances. She hoped their year really *had* been that extraordinary and that Will wasn't losing his well-deserved reputation for frugality.

"Welcome aboard Mr. Connelly and Ms. McCandless-Connelly," the woman—Julia, from Sweden, according to her name badge—said warmly as she handed back Connelly's card. "We set sail in just about three hours. Please, explore the ship and pop into our welcoming reception in the cocktail lounge. I'll have a porter deliver your bags to your suite when your rooms are ready."

"Fantastic," Connelly said, as he tried to slip her a folded bill. As cruising rookies, they'd gotten an earful of advice from their cruising-enthusiast friends and relatives, all of which could be distilled into this one rule: when in doubt, tip.

Julia apparently hadn't gotten the memo. She recoiled and pulled her hand back as if the twenty were a spider. Connelly shot Sasha a questioning look, and she shrugged. She had no idea what the problem was.

The hostess smoothed her face into a pleasant expression and leaned in close. "I'm so sorry, Mr. Connelly. I can't accept a gratuity."

Connelly wrinkled his forehead in confusion.

"I'm afraid I don't understand," Sasha said in an attempt to rescue her husband from what was quickly becoming an awkward social encounter.

"If you don't mind my inquiring, is this your first time cruising with us?" Julia asked.

"It's our first time cruising period," Sasha told her.

Understanding lit in the woman's ice blue eyes. "Ah, I see. And you didn't peruse our materials before selecting our cruise line for your maiden voyage?"

"To be honest, no. The cruise was a gift."

"Oh, what a lovely gift! In that case, the two of you are in for quite a treat. Sacred Lotus differentiates itself from our competitors by offering a truly pampering, luxury experience where your every need is anticipated and your every wish fulfilled."

Even though Sasha harbored a strong suspicion that the words were taken directly from a marketing pamphlet, the hostess somehow managed to imbue them with such emotion and authenticity that they rang true. She found herself nodding along as Julia continued. "Part of that experience is having a full staff available to assist you without the expectation of receiving any gratuities. In fact, tips are strictly prohibited. Sacred Lotus compensates us very generously, I assure you."

"I see." Connelly slid the twenty into his pocket with a sheepish grin.

Julia smiled back at him. "It's an understandable mistake. But the gratuities policy is only one of the ways in which we distinguish ourselves. We also offer all onboard amenities and activities at no extra fee. For instance, you can avail yourself of unlimited services at Chamomile and Chrysanthemum, our award-winning spa, take cooking classes with our master chef, or perhaps visit the pottery studio for lessons. We like to say both the horizons and your opportunities for adventure are limitless on The Water Lily." She wrapped up her spiel then gestured toward the lounge, where several moneyed-looking couples were already circulating, champagne glasses in hand.

"Just how good *was* last year?" Connelly murmured in Sasha's ear.

No kidding.

As Sasha and Connelly headed toward the reception, the hostess called after them. "Oh, Mr. and Mrs. Connelly?"

They turned back to her. "Yes?"

She trotted away from her station to meet them halfway between the ramp and the entrance to the lounge.

"I'm afraid there's one more thing I forgot to mention," Julia said apologetically.

"Oh?" Connelly said.

"Yes, Sacred Lotus also prides itself on offering our guests a truly rejuvenating, relaxing experience. We promise to take you away from the troubles and nuisances of your daily life. To deliver on that promise, we need you to leave behind your responsibilities and worries. So, unlike our competitors, we do not offer unlimited free Internet access. We don't even offer Internet access for an additional fee. We believe the ability to remove yourself from daily life is priceless, worth far more than constant contact is. We don't want you to be checking your emails, answering questions from your stockbroker, or reading unsettling news. This is your escape, your respite. So I'm afraid you may not have realized that you are about to go off the grid, as it were."

Beside her, Sasha could feel Connelly eyeing her with some concern. She may not have done her usual level of research about the cruise line, but she'd known not to assume she'd have reliable email access. She'd told her parents and Will and Naya to contact Connelly in an emergency. For all Julia's cult-like insistence on the value of cutting themselves off from the outside world, Sasha assumed the cruise ship's systems couldn't block whatever technology powered her husband's government-issued Bat-phone.

Julia was still looking at them with a worried expression.

"Of course, I understand." She flashed the woman a smile. "We do have infant twins, though. I assume when we're docked, we'll have some ability, however limited, to make phone calls?"

Julia's forehead relaxed. "Oh, yes," she assured them. "Either through your phone carrier or ours, you will be able to check on your little angels when we're not at sea. And, of course, in the event of a true emergency, a family member or the authorities could reach you through our captain's communication system."

Sasha imagined navigating this part of the conversation was likely the nastiest part of the woman's job. People felt obliged to be reachable. Rich, important people, who were clearly Sacred Lotus's target demographic, believed they had to be accessible all the time.

Not her. Nobody called up their lawyer to chitchat. If someone was trying to reach Sasha McCandless-Connelly, Esquire, they had a problem, a grievance, or a complaint. She was happy to let the world's issues melt away for an entire week.

As long as she could check in on Finn and Fiona and the pets, she was more than willing to sail off on a wave of blissful ignorance.

Connelly nodded at the woman and put his hand on the small of Sasha's back to pilot her toward the cocktail party. "Thanks for the head's up, Julia. I hope we'll see you around the ship."

2.

INA FELT THE Vietnamese man watching her. Man was a bit of an overstatement, she corrected herself. He was more of a teenaged boy, about her age. She'd heard the others call him Binh.

She kept her eyes on the fishing net she was mending and tried to control her heartbeat.

Living on the boat was more stressful than she'd expected it to be. The crew shared cramped living quarters. They slept, during the day, in hammocks that hung haphazardly in the small room below deck where they also stored supplies and ate their meals. She passed her days in constant fear of being found out for a woman.

She peeked up at Binh. He was still watching her with open curiosity on his face. Her hands began to shake, and the large, dirty needle passed into one of the open sores that had developed on her palms. She inhaled sharply and shook her hand as if that would take the sting away.

Everyone on the crew had similar wounds. They never healed because they never dried out. The cuts filled with saltwater and fish slime and developed festering infections.

Binh flicked his eyes around the cramped quarters, confirming that nobody was paying attention then, with a resigned sigh, he put aside the knife he was using to gut the small silver fish and returned the fish to the bucket. He walked softly on his bare feet; in a flash, he was crouched beside her, speaking in low Vietnamese.

She shook her head and answered in her broken Thai, "No understand."

He gestured for her injured hand. She hesitated and gave him a long look. His brown eyes were sad and honest. They reminded her of her father despite the difference in age.

He spoke again. It sounded like he was trying to speak her language, but his Malay was so garbled, she couldn't make it out. She knew what he wanted though.

She held out her palm, still throbbing with pain and infection, and he took it in his own cool, slim hand. He bent his head low and turned her hand this way and that, inspecting the cut. With one smooth, fast motion he reached into a hidden pocket in his raggedy, dirty shorts and produced a small, round tin like a magician. He twisted it open and rubbed white balm over the wound. Her pain began to ease instantly. She made a small moue of surprise and looked up to meet his eyes.

The tin had already vanished, no doubt stowed safely back in his secret hiding place.

"Thank you," she said first in Thai and then in Malay. She wished she knew Vietnamese. He'd shown her the first small kindness anyone on the ship had extended her and she wasn't sure he understood her gratitude.

He blinked then nodded. "Binh." He smiled and pointed at his chest.

"Omar," she answered, giving her father's name and trying to keep her voice low in a coarse, masculine whisper.

He held her eyes for a long moment then said in unmistakable Thai, "Girl."

A shiver of shock ran through her body. She felt herself stiffen. She began to shake her head from side to side. *No, no, no.*

Binh shook his own head and raised his hand. "I won't tell."

Her head fell back against the rough wall and she went limp. She blinked back tears of relief. He was going to keep her secret. She managed a small smile and jabbed her thumb at her chest. "Mina."

He might have said something more, but just then the man who served as second-in-command to the captain clattered down the stairs and began banging on the walls with his stick. It was the signal that it was time to fish.

Mina and Binh scrambled to their feet and fell in with the rest of the crew, jostling their way up the stairs. It didn't pay to be last above deck. The last two men up would be swatted with the stick and tasked with swimming out into the inky ocean to pull in the nets—a dangerous job in the dark of night. Already one man, a Cambodian named Arun, had gotten tangled in the unseen nets and pulled under. Mina knew that his bloated corpse would bob in her nightmares about the sea the next time she closed her eyes. She threw her elbow into the back of the man ahead of her and wriggled in front of him.

~ ~ ~ ~ ~ ~ ~ ~ ~ ~

"Sasha," Connelly called, waving at her from across the room.

She nodded to let him know she'd heard him and excused herself from the conversation with the retired minister and his delightful librarian wife. As she crossed the parquet dance floor, she reached out and snagged a bacon-wrapped scallop from a circulating waiter's silver tray. She popped it in her mouth and swallowed. Then she smiled at her husband and his new friends—a deeply tanned man with a shock of silver hair and a pale, blue-eyed woman not much taller than Sasha herself.

"Doctor Eleanor and Mister Oliver Kurck, this is my wife Sasha McCandless-Connelly."

The woman juggled her plate of cheese cubes into her left hand and extended her right. "Call me Elli. It's a pleasure to meet you."

Sasha shook the woman's hand and noted that it was surprisingly calloused, given her expensive gown and their surroundings. "The pleasure's all mine. What kind of doctor are you—if you don't mind my asking?"

Elli smiled. "I'm a professor of social justice. I teach at the University of Helsinki." She looked down at her hands. "I just finished up some field work teaching my students how to build tents for refugees. I think I need a manicure." Her English was flawless and lightly accented.

"That sounds like important work," Sasha said. "And, I wouldn't worry about your nails. I'm told there's a spa onboard."

"Ah, yes. This is a very posh ship, isn't it? The cruise was Oliver's idea. When he retired from investment banking, he insisted we travel through the exotic parts of Southeast Asia that I never get to see in the course of my research. So, here we are."

Sasha turned to the woman's husband. "Retired? Congratulations."

His voice boomed. "Thank you. Yes, after twenty-seven years at the Nordic Investment Bank, I'm ready for some adventure. I hear from your husband that he, like me, is enjoying his freedom but you're a hard-charging law firm partner."

"More like exhausted mother of twins," she said with a wink.

Elli nodded. "Our children are grown, but I remember those years." She leaned forward, and Sasha caught a whiff of spicy perfume. "Just remember: the days are long, but the years are short."

Sasha was about to respond when Connelly caught her elbow. "If you'll excuse us, I see the captain."

She cocked her head at the abrupt interruption.

Oliver took it upon himself to explain Connelly's weird behavior. "Captain van Metier likes to introduce himself to each of his guests. He'd stopped by to see us while you were chatting with that couple from one of the Dakotas. He made Leo promise to bring you over when you returned."

"North Dakota," she interjected then continued, "Well, it was so nice to meet you both. I hope we—"

"Oh, don't worry you'll see plenty of us," Elli promised. "The husbands have already been making plans. I hope you weren't expecting to have Leo all to yourself during this trip."

Sasha smiled. "I know better. Connelly's a social butterfly. I'll just be glad to have him to myself in bed."

The couple laughed politely as Sasha and Connelly walked toward the captain. Sasha's cheeks burned with embarrassment as she realized belatedly how she sounded.

She turned to Connelly. "Oh my gosh—I didn't mean that the way it came out. I just meant it would be nice not to wake up to feed someone or change a diaper in the middle of the night."

"I know. But you should have seen their expressions." He laughed.

Her flush deepened and she poked him in the ribs with her elbow. "Better behave. The captain might put you in the brig."

The captain was straight out of central casting. Craggy, weathered face, erect military bearing. When Connelly entered his line of vision, he nodded and turned away from the officer he'd been speaking with and pivoted to greet them.

"Captain van Metier," Connelly said, "I'd like to introduce my wife, Sasha McCandless-Connelly."

The captain smiled and gave a formal little bow from his waist as he reached for Sasha's hand and clasped it between his own instead of shaking it. "Ah, Mrs. Connelly, how nice to meet you."

Sasha slipped her hand out of his grasp and smiled. "Captain." She tried not giggle at his anachronistic chivalry. He was definitely the Old-World European sort.

"I'm so glad your husband brought you over. I take my guests' comfort very seriously. I encourage you to bring any concerns or problems that you may encounter to my attention directly, and I will ensure that they are addressed by our top-notch staff to your satisfaction."

Sasha arched an eyebrow. "That's very kind of you, Captain. But I assume you'll be pretty busy piloting the ship, won't you?" Surely the dozens of uniformed staff members could handle any issues short of steering the ship.

He chuckled. "*The Water Lily* is a marvel of technology, Mrs. Connelly. At the risk of talking myself right out of a job, I must admit that computers do most of the driving these days. You'll have to come visit the bridge. It looks like it should be part of your country's space program with all the screens and gadgets, if my memories of my trip to Florida are reliable."

Sasha smiled and cut her eyes back to her husband. The little one-on-one with the captain was a nice touch, but she was ready to find a place to sit down and have something a little more substantial than hors d'oeuvres.

The captain seemed to read her mind.

"The dining venues will be opening shortly. I trust you'll find something appropriately scrumptious to dine on and, please be sure to toast to the voyage with a flute of champagne before we set sail. It's believed to be good luck."

"Well, if I must," Sasha joked.

The captain bowed again, kissed Sasha's hand with a flourish, then turned back to the officer to resume their discussion.

3.

LEO SMILED AND nodded at the cheerful man across the table, who was halfway through his lengthy play-by-play of a cricket match. Leo was only half listening. Most of his attention was on Sasha, who was fading—and fast. She stifled her third yawn in about ten minutes and gave him an apologetic look before turning back to the woman to her left, a schoolteacher from Mexico City.

His five-foot-tall, green-eyed firecracker in three-inch heels was severely sleep deprived. The long hours of lawyering and mothering she'd put in so as to pull off a nine-day absence from her responsibilities had left her depleted. Add in the international travel and the time change—not to mention the fact that she found the coffee in Singapore to be insufferably weak—and it all amounted to a woman about to fall asleep on her feet.

He took a long sip of the velvety, twenty-one-year-old single barrel malt scotch that the waiter had wisely recommended and waited for Raj to pause for a breath. Then he jumped in, "Well, sounds like the Londoners team sure pulled out a daisy cutter! If you'll excuse us, Sasha and I have had a long day with a lot of excitement. We're going to go back to the room and rest." He folded his linen napkin over his dessert plate and pushed back his chair.

Sasha blinked in surprise at his announcement. She checked her watch. "Are you sure? It's not even nine-thirty yet."

He noted the dark half circles under her eyes. "I'm sure."

She made her excuses to the schoolteacher and gave her after-dinner coffee one last wistful glance before circling the table to take his arm.

He bent and spoke in her ear. "I think you need a soft pillow and a warm blanket even more than you need your hit of coffee."

She opened her mouth in what he assumed would be an attempt at a protest, but instead raised her hand to cover yet another little yawn. She gave a rueful laugh. "I guess you're right. Anyway, I spoke to Julia earlier, and she promised to hook me up with some whole beans, a grinder, and a French press in the morning so I can make some coffee that's at least slightly stronger than water."

Why wasn't he surprised?

"Of course you did."

He put his hand on the small of her narrow back to pilot her across the edge of the dance floor. Oliver Kurck twirled Elli in his arms and called out, "Not dancing tonight? Perhaps you're headed to the gaming tables, eh?"

"Oh, no, we're going to call it a night," he answered.

Elli giggled, probably remembering Sasha's earlier remark. "To be sure."

"Good night, friends." And with that, Oliver spun his wife back toward the middle of the dance floor.

"They're cute," Sasha remarked as they turned out of the ballroom and continued along the hallway to the wide stairs leading up to the suites.

"Mmm-hmm," he responded, distracted by the way her hip bumped against his thigh. "I thought you looked like you could use some sleep. But if you'd rather make better use of our time alone..."

His voice trailed off and he gave her a suggestive look.

She peeked up at him from under her long eyelashes. "Mr. Connelly, whatever did you have in mind?"

His pulse quickened. Maybe the evening was going to go a little differently than he thought. He leaned in close. "I'm sure we can think of something."

He mounted the steps behind her, pausing to enjoy the view. She looked over her shoulder at him and giggled. It was right about then that he realized no obstacles in the form of a diaper change, a burping, or a feeding stood between him, his wife, and a king bed piled high with fluffy pillows. He managed to suppress the urge to pump his fist.

When they reached the outer door to their rooms, they bumped into Bruce, their valet—who insisted on calling himself their personal butler— on his way out.

"Mrs. Connelly; Mr. Connelly," he said in his precise British accent as he held the door open, "I've just turned down your bed and left fresh ice and the makings of your nightcap. Please do let me know if you require any other assistance before you retire."

"Thanks so much," Sasha said as she slipped past him and through the open door.

"Yes, thank you, Bruce. But Mrs. Connelly and I have everything we need for the rest of the night. Please see that we're not disturbed until morning." Leo gave him a meaningful look.

Bruce nodded knowingly. "Very good, sir."

Leo followed his wife into the room and locked the deadbolt. Then gathered Sasha into his arms and nuzzled her neck. "Now where were we?"

She gave him a dazzling smile. "I believe we were going to make good use of this magically baby-free night. Will you help me out of this dress?" She turned and lifted her hair off her neck

He lowered her zipper as slowly as he could manage, savoring the moment. The evening gown puddled at her feet and she stepped out of it. He scooped it up and headed for the closet, loosening his tie and unbuttoning his shirt one-handed as he walked.

"Be back in a second," he promised.

Sasha ran her hands along the snow white comforter that stretched across the expanse of the bed. "I'll be right here."

Approximately forty seconds later, he emerged from the closet to find that she was as good as her word. She was right there, all right.

Face down, smack in the middle of the bed, already drooling on one of the silk pillows, her back rising and falling with her deep, even breaths.

Leo shook his head and walked over to the bar to fix himself a drink. He didn't have the heart to wake her.

~ ~ ~ ~ ~ ~ ~ ~ ~ ~ ~

Should he wake her?

Binh gnawed on the jagged skin around his cuticle and thought. As he worried, he kept his eyes on Mina. She was definitely sleeping. Her head lolled back against the splintered wood of the mast and her limp hands hung at her sides.

He'd seen her returning with a load of herring to deposit in the rusted bucket, but then instead of returning to her position on the net, she'd rested her head against the wood and closed her eyes. He understood the need to pause to rest. He was sure she was tired. He was tired. They were all tired.

They fished in the darkness of the night because the silver sparkling fish were easier to see in the black water when the sun wasn't glinting off the waves. And they slept during the heat of the day. But the hammocks were too crowded, the tight space too packed, for everyone to sleep all afternoon. So they took turns napping, grabbing an hour or two, three if they were very fortunate. Unless there were many fish to sort. Then no one slept until the work was done.

The schedule left everyone fatigued and shaky. But that didn't matter. If Captain Vũ happened to come by and catch her sleeping, it would be bad. If she were lucky, she'd be whipped. If she were unlucky ... he shuddered, and his eyes slid involuntarily away from the sleeping girl to the inky water below. The last crew member with bad luck had suffered a bout of pneumonia and been dumped overboard, still wheezing.

Yes, definitely wake her.

He started across the deck, careful not to slip on the boards, which were slick with saltwater and fish guts. As he made his way toward her, the captain rounded the corner and instantly began to bark at him in Vietnamese, angrily ordering Binh back to his spot at the net. He ducked his head and scurried as quickly as he dared across the wet floor. He didn't dare defy a direct order. He couldn't risk it.

When he'd first learned that the captain was Vietnamese, too, he thought for a moment he might receive kinder treatment than the others. He'd been wrong. It was almost as if Captain Vũ reserved the worst treatment for his countrymen. Binh's rice bowl often contained no fish. It sometimes contained roaches—too often to be a coincidence. He was reprimanded for being too slow, for being clumsy, for accidentally putting a mackerel in the bucket for sardines. Every transgression, no matter how minor, earned Binh a lashing. He winced at the memory, and the deep scars that crisscrossed his back seemed to ache more than usual. He trod to his position at the enormous mesh net and stared unblinkingly down into the churning water.

Afraid to glance back at the sleeping girl, he kept his eyes fixed on the black sea. But his lips moved wordlessly as he repeated a silent mantra: *Wake up, Mina. Wake up, Mina. Please wake up.*

4.

The Gulf of Thailand

BINH WAS DOZING when the sound of a woman screaming penetrated his dream. He jolted awake, his arms and legs jerking, and swiveled his head wildly, looking for the source of the noise. It could only be Mina. She had to stop— quickly, right now—before the unmistakably feminine sound revealed the truth about her.

He scrambled to his feet. He had to find her and plead with her to stop before she got herself in trouble. He raced toward the sound of the screaming coming from below deck. When he reached the top of the stairs, he stopped in his tracks. Captain Vũ had a fistful of Mina's thin white T-shirt and was dragging her up the stairs. She fell to her knees and pleaded in rapid-fire Malay that Binh doubted the captain understood any more than he did, but the tone made her message clear: she was begging for her life. Captain Vũ's face was red, redder than blood, and his mouth was set in a hard slash. He yanked her roughly, her shins banging against the steps.

Binh shrank back against the wall, pressing himself into the wood in an effort not to draw the captain's attention. At this point there was nothing he could do for the girl—she was going to be punished, and given Captain Vũ's naked hatred for him, intervening on her behalf would only make it worse for both of them. All he could do was hope she didn't say his name when she passed by and drag him into her mess. He pinned his eyes to the ground as the captain and his captive clattered up the stairs. But he was unable to stop himself from sneaking a glance at her as she passed him.

Mina was pale with fright and pulling against the captain's grip with all her might, but she gave no indication that she recognized him or thought that anyone might help her. Boys and men stopped what they were doing and poured out from every crevice of the ship to gather on the mid-deck and watch the spectacle in a mixture of horror and anticipation. The captain ignored them all and continued to march, ramrod straight, toward his office with Mina in tow.

When they were several feet away, Binh spotted the red bloom of menstrual blood staining the back of her shorts and he knew that her gender had been revealed before she screamed. He made a silent wish that Captain Vũ would be merciful and that her beating would be quick. Wide awake now and with a sour taste in his mouth, he wandered aimlessly along the deck. His crew mates were chattering in excitement at the novelty of a woman on the ship.

Binh shifted from hoping the captain would deliver a light beating to fervently praying he kept her locked up in one of the cages reserved for troublemakers, if only for her own protection. Many of these men had been at sea for months. Some, like the Cambodians, said they'd been on the water for years. Binh didn't know how long he'd been on the ship. In the beginning, he scratched a line into the floorboards near the kitchen at the end of each day; but after receiving a particularly brutal beating, he decided he no longer wanted to know how long it had been.

There were a lot of men on the ship who had not had the company of a woman in a very long time. Mina's worst punishment might come if she were released back to the crew.

For many hours, Binh thought the universe had answered his request. After Captain Vũ dragged Mina out of sight and into his office, she didn't reemerge. The adrenaline rush of the scene died as quickly as it had flared, and the crew turned back to their work.

Binh sat with a small group and repaired nets. After a while, the round-cheeked Burmese man who called himself Thiha Bo said that he'd caught a glimpse of Mina, crouching in the cage nearest the door.

"What will he do with her?" Binh asked in Thai, a language he was picking up out of necessity.

Thiha Bo rolled his shoulders and didn't offer any guesses.

But the Cambodian with the deep scar bisecting his left cheek rasped, "Probably dump her at the next port. She's no use to him." His gaze grew dreamy. "Too bad. I know I could make good use of her."

The others laughed, but hot anger roiled in Binh's belly and salty tears pricked his eyes. He blinked back the tears and balled his hands into fists but said nothing. After several moments, when he could trust himself to speak, he said, "What's the next port? Songkhla?"

The Cambodian narrowed his eyes and thought. Then he shook his head. "No. Samut Prakan."

Thiha Bo nodded his agreement.

"Malaysia?" Binh asked as a small green bud of hope bloomed in him. The girl was from Malaysia. If Captain Vũ abandoned her near her home, maybe she'd make it back.

"Thailand," the Cambodian informed him with some disgust.

Binh knew he should have a better sense of where they traveled—he'd made the circuit multiple times. But each voyage, the same disorientation overcame him. The miles of endless water washed away the landmarks in his mind's eye. He never knew where they'd been or where they were headed. He was always turned around, confused. He wished he could fix a map in his brain. Maybe then he could plan his escape when they were nearing Phu My or another port near his home. Maybe a fellow Vietnamese would wander past the ship and agree to buy his freedom. He'd heard stories like that. But he just drifted from port to port in a constant seasick daze, and his hopes for himself grew smaller and dimmer each day. Now he would hope for Mina, he told himself.

He returned his attention to the mesh netting in his lap. They needed to fix all the nets before nightfall. The captain had given the word that they would fish again tonight.

5.

The Gulf of Thailand

SASHA STARED UP at the ceiling, wide-eyed. Beside her, Connelly slept, his breathing even, deep, slow. She shifted onto her side and willed herself back to sleep.

It wasn't going to happen.

She'd always been a light sleeper and, thankfully, didn't require much more than five solid hours to function. Of course, since the twins' birth, five uninterrupted hours of sleep had moved from the 'doable' category to the 'you wish' category. And here she was—finally able to sleep all she wanted—suffering from insomnia.

She pushed herself up on one elbow and checked the time on the bedside table: 4:20 A.M., local time. She groaned, flopped back into the cloud-like pillow, and glared at her slumbering husband as if it were all his fault that her body clock was going haywire. He, on the other hand, had somehow magically reset his circadian rhythm before their plane had touched down in Singapore.

Grumbling under her breath at the unfairness of it all, she slid out from under the light blanket and stood. She stretched her back and took several deep breaths then peeked through the sliding glass doors. The sky was still dark, but she didn't think it would be long before the sun started its slow climb over the horizon. She padded to the closet and eased open the door. She dressed silently and quickly, choosing her running clothes mainly by feel, and hoped the shorts and top she selected kind of, sort of matched—or at least didn't clash too badly. She tried to remember if she'd packed anything particularly colorful but drew a blank.

She crouched and laced up her shoes then pulled her hair into a ponytail. She closed the closet door soundlessly and scooped up her cruise card. With a final, backward glance at Connelly, who had rolled into the dead center of the bed and was stretched out, still sleeping soundly, she disengaged the door lock and crept out of the room.

The chill of the ocean breeze stung her eyes and she blinked a few times before filling her lungs with the crisp, salty air and heading down the stairs to the Promenade Deck. When she'd asked Bruce if there was a running track onboard, he'd recommended that she run on one of the fitness center's fancy, technology-laden treadmills, which offered everything from a heart rate monitor and flat-screen television to a panoramic view of the Gulf of Thailand from the uppermost Sun Deck, but she preferred to run outside when she could. So he'd directed her to the Promenade Deck and told her three laps would equal a mile. She had plenty of energy to burn; she just hoped she wouldn't get dizzy running in circles.

Fifteen laps, a quick five miles, she promised herself. Then she could go brew some of the amazing coffee that Julia had procured, seemingly by magic.

Spurred on by the thought of strong, hot coffee, she glanced up toward the sky. It was still navy blue and starry, although a faint light was beginning to glow below the horizon. She filled her lungs with air and started running. About a quarter of the way through her first lap, she hit her stride, her arms and legs pumping in rhythm. She found running oddly relaxing as she took in the views and sounds around her. She never listened to music or podcasts when she ran. Will, who logged his miles on a treadmill while listening to audiobooks of biographies, called her a purist. But the simple truth was she was too aware of the dangers of being disconnected from her surroundings to ever want to risk zoning out while she ran.

She scanned the deck, looking for a stray metal staff that could be pressed into service in the event of a fight or a doorway that might conceal an assailant. She made note of alcoves she could hide in if she needed to evade an attacker and stairs that could lead to escape. After all the years of practicing Krav Maga, she wasn't about to lower her guard just because she was on a cruise. In fact, she'd read that the crime rate on cruise lines was surprisingly high. If she had to guess, she imagined it was precisely because civilians on vacation wanted to relax and bliss out. She huffed out a laugh as she ticked off one full lap in her mind: there was no worry that she and Connelly would grow so laid back they'd fall prey to an onshore pickpocket or room charge scam from a fellow cruiser. Even surrounded by opulence and luxury, she knew they would both remain vigilant—it was an occupational necessity for him, a lifelong habit for her.

Although she stayed alert as she circled the deck, she did allow her mind to wander just a bit. Her thoughts turned to her babies, who were losing their babyness surprisingly quickly. In just six short weeks, they'd be turning one, and, already, she could see them morphing into tiny, little people. Each time they pulled themselves up on the furniture, opened a cabinet door, or rolled a ball back and forth between one another, she saw a flash of personality. It was amazing to think that they would soon be talking to her and Connelly, sharing ideas, dreams, and, if they were anything like her nieces and nephews, telling truly stupid, unfunny jokes. She smiled to herself.

Her mind turned to her active caseload. She got some of her best and most strategic ideas while she was running. She went on for several laps, testing out and rejecting causes of action for her newest case—a class action against a local car dealership for violations of the Truth in Lending Act. At the beginning of each new lap, she paused for a breath to admire the changes in the lightening sky.

She was three quarters of the way through her thirteenth circuit around the deck when she noticed that her right shoe had come untied. She propped her leg up on the railing and leaned forward to tie her shoelace, working in a quick stretch while she was at it. After double knotting the offending lace, she switched legs and stretched her left against the railing as well.

As she straightened, a flaring light in the distance caught her eye. The report of gunfire followed, the sound oddly flat across the sea. Her heart jumped. The sound was so distant, she knew that she was in no immediate danger. Instead of seeking cover, she instinctively leaned forward over the railing and strained to see where the muzzle flash had come from. She spotted a small boat rocking gently in the distance, several miles away. In the weak light, the shadowy figures moving around on the deck of the boat were featureless and genderless. She counted three shapes.

She grasped the top railing and climbed so that she was standing on the middle rail. She held tight and leaned even further over the rail, trying to shrink the distance between her and the other boat. The wind carried the sound of muffled laughter from the boat. Her brain registered confusion at the combination of gunfire and laughing. She might have considered the dissonance longer, but one of the figures raised an arm and moved forward toward the smallest of the three.

Two quick muzzle flashes, two cracks of a gun firing, and then a woman's high-pitched scream filled the air. The screaming continued, louder and urgent, and then the woman was falling, arms wind-milling, as she plunged backward into the water below the boat. Sasha gasped and unthinkingly reached for her throat with one hand. She lost her balance on the slick metal railing and quickly grabbed hold again, steadying herself. She stared at the point in the water where the woman had entered the ocean, but there was no splashing, no calling for help, no arms flailing wildly. There was nothing. After a moment she heard distant male voices raised in the sort of excited celebration she associated with touchdowns, not murders.

She lowered herself back to the deck and shakily sat down in one of the Adirondack chairs arranged in a row nearby. She almost couldn't believe that she'd just witnessed a murder. But the sour taste in her mouth and her shaking hand told her that she had.

She straightened herself, relaxed her shoulders, and forced herself to breathe. Once her heart rate had slowed to something close to normal, she pushed herself up and ran toward the observation deck in search of an officer. She didn't notice the watercolor sunrise painting the sky.

6.

EREK LOOKED OVER his shoulder. Austin was lounging against the mast, chatting with the captain like he didn't have a care in the world.

"Austin, man, come on. The resupply boat's about to leave. We gotta go," Derek urged.

Austin threw him a look of pure disdain. "Don't get your panties in a bunch, McGraw. It's not like he's gonna leave without us."

"Well, he might. He's gotta get that fish to the refrigeration unit like now."

Derek had no idea whether that was true. But what he did know was he didn't like hanging around a boat where they'd just killed a teenaged girl. He wanted to get as far away as possible, as fast as possible, from Vũ and his fishing boat. Especially because nobody had mentioned the freaking cruise ship that was no more than ten miles away. How many potential witnesses were on that thing? He didn't even want to think about it. He shouldn't have had to think about something like that—it was beyond sloppy to call in a hit when there was a ship so close. But Vũ had obviously panicked; and Derek would have bet a month's pay that he hadn't told Thale that he was in populated waters.

Derek had even suggested that Vũ could put some distance between them and the cruise ship first, but Austin had argued that in another hour the sun would be high in the sky. It was better to have the poor light of dawn for cover. Besides, the rich gasbags on the cruise ship were probably all still sleeping off their lobsters and champagne. So, yeah, fine, he'd gone along with it. But now it was time to split.

Austin narrowed his eyes and stared at Derek like he was reading his mind. "Gah, you're always such a punk. What's your hurry to get back there? Think you're missing something?"

Derek knew exactly why Austin was dragging his feet. The armory was brutal. There was nothing to do but lift weights and get into petty fights with the other 'independent contractors.' Derek didn't understand exactly why the floating arsenal always had such a volatile, crappy atmosphere, but it did. He'd have thought that since most of them were former military and had been through basic training, they'd be more than used to cooling their heels while waiting to be called in to action. But, unlike the military, there was no discipline, no structure, no nothing really—just contraband liquor, a boatload of guns and ammunition, and sour, bored men, none of whom were making any money by sitting on the barge. Instead, it was the opposite. They had to pay a daily rate for their spaces, which ate into their earnings and further frayed their nerves. As a result, there was plenty of fighting and little else. While Derek understood all that, it still didn't mean that it was good idea to hang around a crime scene.

"Suit yourself. I'm leaving."

Austin waved a hand at him. "What's the matter, Derek? Afraid mommy'll get mad if you miss your curfew?"

"Come or don't come," he snapped and started across the deck.

Behind him, he could hear Austin wheedling Captain Vũ to let them stay on the boat as permanent security. Derek didn't stop, but he did slow his step and turn to see Vū's reaction to the suggestion. *That* would be a good, and lucrative, gig.

But Vū was shaking his head vigorously while spitting and pointing. "No, no. You go. Too much money, too much money," he said in his broken English.

Derek wasn't surprised. The fleet owner paid them by the incident. It really only made financial sense to call out the 'bodyguards,' as they were euphemistically known, when there was an issue.

"Ah, man, come on," Austin said halfheartedly. He was already starting to follow Derek toward the ramp down to the resupply boat.

Vu was still sputtering, "Go, go. Get out."

"You're welcome," Austin snarked over his shoulder.

Derek could see his point there, too. Here they had just solved Captain Vū's crisis of letting a female sneak onto his boat and this is the thanks he gave—kicking them off unceremoniously. He turned back to tell Austin to forget about Vū because he had a bottle of cheap vodka hidden in his footlocker when he caught motion out of the corner of his eye.

Derek froze and peered into the darkness of the stairs leading down to the disgusting crew quarters below deck.

Austin stepped behind him, "What's up, man?" he whispered.

Derek put a finger to his lip and kept his eyes locked on the stairway. Vū had insisted his crew was too cowardly to try to intervene on behalf of the girl. But what if they'd gotten up their courage and were planning an ambush? He heard a rustling and reached for his Glock. After a second, a scrawny rat scurried past the base of the stairs, its claws clicking against the wood.

He exhaled and relaxed his grip then shook his head. "It's just a rat. Let's get out here."

Austin didn't argue.

As they boarded the resupply boat, Derek's gaze was pulled as if by a magnet to the spot where the girl entered the water. The surface was calm, like glass. The sharks hadn't found her body yet.

7.

REATHLESS, SASHA convinced the first officer to take her to Captain van Metier. As they raced through the gleaming corridors of the observation deck, she had to admit the captain's assessment of his ship's technology hadn't been far off. It really did look as though one could control a space shuttle from here. They sped past rows of monitors and bright-eyed young ship's officers chattering into headsets while their fingers clattered over keyboards and found the captain standing on the bridge surveying the ocean with his steely gaze. He held a china mug of what looked to be English breakfast tea in his hand.

"Sir," the first mate began, "Mrs. Connelly would like to speak with you urgently."

The captain turned and eyed them both coolly. "Regarding?" His expression conveyed mild curiosity and just a hint of irritation at being bothered.

The first mate, a freckled kid whose name tag identified him as Liam Davidson, stammered, "She said it was for your ears only, sir."

The captain held his gaze for a moment, making plain his views about that answer before turning to Sasha. "I see. Mrs. Connelly, now you have my ears. What can I do for you?"

Sasha cleared her throat and reminded herself speak as calmly as she could. "I'd really rather not say in front of Officer Davidson. It's a private matter."

The captain's silver eyebrows meandered up his forehead and an expression of discomfort flashed across his face. "If this is a female matter, our medical officer has—"

"No, it's nothing like that," she explained, resisting the urge to tell him she knew how to handle her 'female matters.' "It's a criminal matter, actually."

She apparently said the magic words because the captain nodded curtly to dismiss Davidson. The young officer wasted no time beating his retreat.

As soon as he was out of earshot, the captain asked, "What sort of criminal matter?"

Sasha nodded. "I went for a run on the Promenade Deck and I saw something." Her voice faltered, and she took a moment to steady it before going on. "Something on the ocean."

A smidgeon of relief registered in the captain's eyes when he realized that whatever she'd seen hadn't happened on the ship. "I see. What exactly did you witness?"

Sasha didn't see any point in sugarcoating the news. "A murder."

He blinked but otherwise didn't react visibly. "A murder," he repeated.

"Yes. Out there." Sasha turned and scanned the ocean, trying to find the boat in the distance. "There! Do you see that speedboat or whatever that is? Just behind it, there's another vessel. It happened right there."

He frowned and looked where she pointed then swapped his cup of tea for a pair of high-powered binoculars. He surveyed the ocean for a moment and then lowered the binoculars. "That's not a speedboat. It's a resupply ship. The fishing fleets use them to retrieve the catch from the fishing vessels and take it back to land while also bringing in supplies for the crew. This enables the fishing vessels to stay at sea longer which is more cost effective and efficient for the fleets. There's nothing untoward at all about this."

"But someone was killed on the fishing boat," she insisted.

The captain shook his head. "That's not possible, Mrs. Connelly."

Anger bloomed in Sasha's belly; she forced herself to tamp it down. Exploding now would be counterproductive. She needed to convince the captain to radio the authorities. The only way to do that was to stay calm. "I know what I saw," she said in a firm but polite voice. "I saw two men shoot a girl, and she fell into the water."

"A girl?"

"Yes, a girl. Or a woman. I don't know how old she was, but she was definitely a she."

He clasped his hands behind his back and gave her a grandfatherly look. "You must be mistaken. Women aren't permitted on the fishing vessels for a variety of reasons. It's simply not allowed. In all my years of sailing in this part of the world, I assure you I have never seen a woman on a fishing vessel in the Gulf of Thailand."

She stared at him in disbelief. He really wasn't going to do anything about it. She switched tacks. "Well, even if I *am* mistaken, *something* happened on that boat. I know what a muzzle flash looks like and I know the sound of gunfire. Why don't you just call the authorities and let them look into it?"

The captain's genial mask slipped. "With all due respect, I'm not going to bother the authorities and risk falling behind our sailing schedule over a couple of fishermen having fun shooting at fish in the water—an activity that may not be strictly legal or advisable, but one that is certainly not worth wasting the time of either law enforcement or our passengers."

She responded in her best litigator voice, "I just want to be sure that I understand. What you're telling me is that you refuse to pass along a passenger's report of a possible murder. Is that correct?"

He took his time answering. "What I'm telling you is that you simply did not witness a murder."

She fixed him with her most withering look—the one she usually reserved for sexist opposing attorneys and busybody mothers offering unsolicited advice on the playground. He flinched but didn't back down.

"I know what I saw," she insisted again, careful to keep her tone even and her pitch low, even though she wanted to shriek in his face and flail her arms around frantically. Her instincts told her

Captain Jan van Metier would waste no time dismissing her as a hysterical woman.

Now he arranged his concrete face into something that approximated a smile. "The eyes can play tricks on you at sea. I assure you, Mrs. Connelly, if someone had fallen overboard from a nearby vessel, an SOS call would have come across the radio. One did not. Now, if you'll excuse me, I am quite busy. Perhaps you would enjoy some roulette in the casino or, better yet, a massage in the spa. I'm sure it would help relieve your stress."

He turned on his heel and left her standing at the bridge. She scanned the white-capped waves below, as if she might miraculously spot the girl. Futile, she knew. That girl was dead, sinking below the ocean's surface—and not because she'd fallen overboard. Sasha had witnessed it: the push; the cries; the quick flash of guns; the small shape falling into the water; then the burbled scream that faded; and, lastly, the men's laughter that hung on the sea air.

She rubbed her arms vigorously to warm herself from the chill that settled over her and took one last, long look at the water. The small boat that the woman had been pushed from grew even smaller. If she squinted, though, she could still make out its shape in the vast ocean. And the resupply boat was just a dot near the horizon.

She stared at the ocean for a moment. Then she jutted out her chin and set off to find Connelly. Captain van Metier could blow her off, but she'd like to see him try that with her hulking federal agent of a husband.

~ ~ ~ ~ ~ ~ ~ ~ ~ ~

Leo gathered his wife into his arms. Her shoulders shook against his chest. He didn't know whether she was trembling from the horror of what she had witnessed, her anger at not being believed, or some combination of the two. All he knew was that he needed to comfort her and then deal with that idiot of a captain.

"Hey, hey," he soothed, "you're okay. It's okay."

She took a shuddering breath then looked up at him. Her green eyes were troubled. "I saw a murder."

"I'm sorry."

"But you believe me?"

"Of course I believe you." He did, and not only because plenty of classified briefings detailing murder on the high seas had crossed his desk over the years. He believed her because she wasn't prone to histrionics—if anything, she was the op-posite.

Her body relaxed against his. "Thank you." She paused a beat. "But we have to do something."

He smoothed a hand over her hair, still damp from her run, then squeezed her narrow shoulder. "You take a long, hot shower. Leave Captain van Metier to me."

She smiled weakly.

Leo knew she loathed having to ask for help. She hated appearing needy almost as much as she hated being dismissed on the basis of her gender or her size. But she was realistic enough to know that sometimes it took a caveman to persuade a caveman. And for all his evolved, modern sensibili-ties, Leo Connelly was perfectly capable of being a caveman when the situation warranted.

Sasha gave him a quick peck on the cheek and headed toward the bathroom. "A hot shower does sound like heaven."

"Good. Then when I come back, we'll have some coffee and plan the rest of our day." He snatched up his key card from the bedside table and grabbed a jacket from the back of the chair in the living ar-ea. He paused by the door. "Don't forget to lock this behind me. You don't want Bruce to get an eyeful."

She laughed for a second, but then her tone grew serious again. "Hey, babe?"

He turned to face her.

"Did you happen to bring your gun?"

He kept his face neutral even though the question revealed just how deeply rattled she was. They had struck an uneasy truce around the subject of whether he was carrying his weapon outside the house. It was a don't ask, don't tell sort of policy. In their home, by agreement, his Glock was secured in the gun safe at all times. But sometimes he deemed it advisable to conceal carry when he was out on the street. But an international cruise that involved clearing customs at the Singapore airport and multiple ports of entry throughout Southeast Asia was not one of those times. He'd talked to Hank, and they'd agreed getting the appropriate clearances would raise more questions than he was comfortable with given the unofficial nature of his job—not to mention the unofficial status of the entire department Hank ran. He looked at Sasha for a long moment before answering. "No, I didn't bring it. But don't worry."

She shot him a look. "Who said I was worried?" She tossed the question over her shoulder and strode toward the bathroom.

Her bravado made his heart ache just a little.

8.

AN VAN METIER felt the dull throb of the very beginning of a headache just behind his right temple. He was not surprised. His morning had gone poorly, to put it mildly. First, there had been the hysterical visit from the Connelly woman. Then her oaf of a husband had burst on the observation deck demanding to see him.

He rolled his shoulders to release some of the stress he'd been holding since the confrontation with Mr. Connelly. The American had blustered and threatened and, in general, had behaved as Americans tended to behave—ordering him to contact shore side authorities and making vague statements about how important he was back home. Jan had maintained his diplomatic demeanor, but it had taken all of his self-control. How dare a civilian passenger presume to tell him what to do. He was the captain of this vessel. He made the decisions. He gave the orders.

For a brief second, he thought longingly of his time in the Royal Netherlands Navy. The military life may have lacked the softness and the luxury of his current assignment, but at least in the navy everyone knew his place.

Jan had almost no doubt that Mrs. Connelly *had* witnessed a murder. But there was no margin in letting her, or her self-important husband, know that. He planned to continue to maintain that the very idea was laughable.

But he was not laughing. The moment she'd told him what she'd seen, he'd suspected a Thale vessel was involved. And the presence of the resupply boat had added to his belief. Those ships did, as he'd told Mrs. Connelly, bring supplies to the boats and take away the fish the crews had caught. But what he hadn't mentioned to her was that they also served as an informal taxi service for the armed mercenaries who lived on the floating armory just north of Kuala Lumpur—and Thale was known to be an enthusiastic purchaser of their services.

Finally, to compound the situation, in his efforts to assuage Mr. Connelly's concerns, he'd enlarged a still of the shipping boat taken by one of cruise liner's many security cameras. The pixilated shot showed an empty deck, which hadn't really satisfied Mr. Connelly, who argued that the fact the picture showed nothing untoward happening at that precise moment was proof of nothing.

For Jan, though, it was proof of something. It confirmed that the ship in the blurry photograph was part of the fleet owned and operated by the powerful Thale Group. In addition to its fishing enterprise, the family behind Thale owned most of the port city of Samut Prakan. They owned the bars, the girls, the restaurants, the fishmongers, and the local police. Although Thale's ships were flagged out of Cambodia, the company had a finger in just about every pie in Thailand from the legal enterprises to the more lucrative, illegal ones. Crossing Thale would be suicidal, probably in a literal sense.

Just thinking about it made his headache bloom in full force. He checked the time: in just a few hours they would dock in Laem Chabang. The itinerary called for an overnight stay, so that the passengers could travel north to the city of Bangkok for an excursion, which meant that he could blow off a little steam of his own.

In the meantime, he deleted the photograph and erased the video footage that showed the shipping vessel. He knew the materials weren't truly gone and could no doubt be restored by specialists, but at least they weren't just sitting out there for anyone who cared to see them.

His sipped his tea, which was now quite cold, and willed the hands on his watch to move more quickly.

9.

ONNELLY CAME back to the room just as Bruce arrived bearing a tray of fresh fruit and muffins. Sasha unbolted the door and let them both into the main living area of the suite. Bruce immediately set up the breakfast goodies while Sasha brewed the coffee herself. She liked Bruce—a lot—but there was just no way she was going to trust a tea-drinking Brit to make her cup of morning joe. She wondered idly if that made her a xenophobe, but then decided she really didn't trust *anyone* not a blood relative or bound to her by marriage with the first cup of the day. After that first one, though, she'd let the devil himself make her coffee.

She almost laughed at herself, but one look at Connelly's dark expression stopped her mid-giggle. She could tell that she wasn't going to like what he'd have to report.

She was itching to know what happened, but she held her tongue while Bruce finished setting up the breakfast.

"Can I get you anything else at the moment?" the valet asked.

"No thank you." Connelly's voice was tight.

Bruce nodded and walked out of the suite.

Sasha crossed the room to hand her husband a mug of steaming coffee. "It went that well?"

He took the coffee in both hands and gave her a grim look. "The good news is Captain van Metier didn't blow you off because you're a woman."

She couldn't believe it. "He didn't take you seriously either?"

"Not even a little bit."

They sipped their coffee in silence.

After a moment, she picked up a fork, pushed some berries around her plate listlessly, and then dropped the fork with a clatter. "Now what? We can't do nothing."

His expression mirrored her frustration. He answered slowly. "I really hate to do this, but I think we need to reach out to Hank."

Sasha felt some of her tension ease as a frisson of relief ran along her spine. She'd hoped he'd say that, but she hadn't wanted to be the one to suggest it. Even now she wasn't exactly clear about Hank's role in the Department of Homeland Security, let alone her own husband's. Involving Hank wasn't her first option, either, but it seemed to be the best.

"Okay," she agreed. "Go get your secret agent phone, and let's see if we can reach out to him." Connelly hesitated. He checked the time and did a quick calculation. "It's pretty late there. We might wake the kids."

"It's Hank. Just because he's a single dad to half a dozen children doesn't mean the man's going to turn his cell phone off after dinner," she pointed out.

"I know. But ... still."

She understood his reluctance. The instant they'd become parents their own obsession with being available twenty-four hours a day, seven days a week, suddenly seemed ill-advised, if not insane. They both tried hard to leave work behind at the end of the workday and only responded to true emergencies after-hours. But she was fairly certain the murder of a young woman in international waters constituted an emergency.

"I think it's okay to call him. Really." She picked her fork back up and speared some blueberries.

Connelly opened the drawer by his side of the bed and removed his government-issued satellite phone. She ate some fruit salad and picked at a muffin while he placed the international call. Hank answered almost immediately, and Connelly put him on speakerphone.

"Hank, it's Leo and Sasha. We're sorry to bother you this late at night, but something's come up," Connelly began.

Hank's voice was full of concern. "What do you mean, 'something's come up'? What could come up? Aren't you supposed to be on your cruise?"

"Oh, we're on the cruise," Sasha assured him.

"You mean to tell me that you two managed to get yourselves into trouble in the middle of the ocean?" Hank's tone suggested that his disbelief was completely feigned.

"Something like that," Connelly said. "Sasha, why don't you tell Hank what you saw?"

She took a steadying breath before plunging into her story. "I was having trouble sleeping this morning, so I went for a very early run. The sun hadn't quite come up yet, so there wasn't really anyone else up and about." She began slowly, but as she recounted the scene, her cadence increased until she was almost breathless and she had to force herself to slow down. "I stopped to tie my shoe, and I saw a flash of light out on the water—"

"A flash? What kind of flash? You haven't run into any unidentified flying objects out there, have you?" He chuckled.

She wished she'd seen little green men from Mars. That would have been a welcome alternative to the reality. "It was a muzzle flash." She paused and let that information sink in.

"You're sure?"

She swallowed around the lump in her throat, but before she could answer, Connelly said, "She's sure."

"I heard the gunfire," she went on, "and then I heard screaming—a woman screaming. There was more gunfire, then she plunged into the water from the deck of what is apparently a small fishing boat."

Connelly reached over, covered her hands with his, and gave a gentle squeeze.

When Hank spoke again, all the humor had drained from his voice. "You witnessed a murder?"

"Right. Now, granted, the boat was some distance away, and the light was bad, but I know what I saw." Even to herself, she sounded defensive—like a deponent who'd been backed into a corner by sharp questioning. She was still feeling the sting of the captain's dismissal. She looked at Connelly helplessly.

He explained, "Sasha reported it to the ship's captain and he basically blew her off as a hysterical woman. I went to talk to him and didn't get much further. He insists she couldn't have seen what she saw and refuses to call the authorities. So, what's our play?"

Hank's voice rumbled, "Where are you, exactly?"

Connelly looked her. "I'm not sure, exactly. We're somewhere in the Gulf of Thailand. We dock this afternoon at some regional port for an overnight."

"Is the port in Bangkok?"

"No, Bangkok's about two hours to the north. I can't remember the name of the seaside town where we dock."

Connelly rifled through the welcome materials that Bruce had given them on the first day. "It's called Laem Chabang," he supplied. "Why?"

"Can you get to Bangkok?" Hank wanted to know.

"Sure, the cruise line arranged an excursion, actually. But we were thinking we'd find a local guide to take us—you know, get a more authentic look at the town. Why?"

"There's a Legat in Bangkok," Hank answered.

'A Legat?' Sasha mouthed toward her husband.

"An FBI Legal Attaché who's assigned to the U.S. Embassy in Bangkok," Connelly explained. "Their focus is principally on terrorism, though. Doesn't this sound more like a local law enforcement issue, Hank?"

"Maybe. But the Legats also liaise with local law enforcement organizations and security departments in their host countries. You're not going to get anywhere by walking in off the street and reporting it to the police station at Laem Chabang—assuming there even is one. And we don't know if the shooter, the victim, or anyone involved is a Thai national. They'll have no reason to get involved—unless the Legat asks them to," Hank answered.

Sasha piped up. "Actually, I'm pretty sure that authority to investigate will depend on where that fishing boat is registered. If I recall my maritime law correctly, criminal activity at sea is governed largely by a series of international treaties that only bind the signatories."

"And you know all this maritime law stuff, how?" Hank's voice crackled over the phone.

Sasha glanced at Connelly, whose expression conveyed mild interest, as if he shared his boss's curiosity.

She searched her mind for a plausible explanation. Why would a litigator specializing in complex commercial disputes have a working knowledge about the Jones Act and related arcane admiralty law topics? *Pittsburgh does have three rivers; I thought it might come in handy?* No, not really believable.

Meanwhile, the international call was probably costing a small fortune and they were in danger of losing their signal at any moment. She sighed and settled on the truth. "I had a crush on the professor who taught admiralty law," she mumbled.

Of course in reality, Professor Alfredson's class lectures were geared more to the maritime equivalent of Worker's Compensation cases, cases involving collisions between vessels, and the ever popular negligent damage or loss of cargo. They rarely touched on anything quite so esoteric as multi-jurisdictional criminal law. But the professor had written about the topic extensively, and Sasha had been lucky enough to edit an article he'd written for the law review.

Back on land, Hank chuckled. Beside her, Connelly rolled his eyes.

"Figures. I'll bet he was a young intellectual type. Hair to his collarbone, horn-rimmed glasses. Rode his bike to class," he cracked.

She arched an eyebrow. "He was a mostly bald widower and grandfather in his seventies. He wore Hickey Freeman suits and drove his Volvo wagon to class. He *did* have horn-rimmed glasses."

Hank and Connelly both dissolved into laughter.

Connelly shook his head. "Attracted to his intellect, huh?"

She drew herself up to her full, if meager, height. "As a matter of fact, I was. Tastes change, though. Look at me now. Married to an empty-headed pretty boy."

He broke into a wide grin. She felt her own mouth curving into a mirroring smile. For a fleeting moment, safe in their small cabin, they could laugh.

Hank cleared his throat then brought them back to the purpose of the call. "Let's not overlawyer this problem. When you witness a crime, you should report it. The fact that your ship's captain wants to turn a blind eye is a bit troubling."

"I don't think it's anything nefarious. I think he's somewhat of a sexist, and he's more concerned with staying on schedule and delivering the high-quality, luxury experience his passengers expect than with seeing justice done for some nameless woman," she responded.

"Hmph," Hank grumped in response. "Well, let me make some calls. I'll be back in touch when I have a contact for you."

"Thanks," Sasha and Connelly said in unison before ending the call.

"Now what?" Connelly asked.

She let a slow smile play across her lips. "I was thinking we could do something ... life affirming." She looked meaningfully toward the bedroom. He dropped his blueberry muffin as if it were radioactive and raced her to the bed.

10.

BINH LAY IN his ragged hammock. It swayed in time with the ocean's gentle movement. He stared sightlessly at the beams above his head.

It was the hottest part of the day, time to sleep. But he knew that sleep would elude him. His heart was still hammering, even now all these hours later, from the near miss on the stairway. He'd been so lucky: the rodent skittered across the floor at the most fortunate time. He didn't want to think about what might have happened if the shooters had caught him peering up the stairs.

Then he caught himself. *Don't be stupid, Binh.*

He knew exactly what would've happened if they'd caught him. He'd have shared Mina's fate.

Mina. Her terrified screams still filled his ears, and the echo of the sound tore through him. There was nothing he could have done to save her. Once Captain Vũ had called his bosses and told them there was a woman on the ship, her fate had been sealed.

A roach crabbed its way up Binh's arm. He shifted and flicked it to the ground. He knew that he'd possessed no more power to help the girl than did that bug.

Although he hadn't been able to help her, she—in death—would help him. He vowed to find some way off the boat. It didn't matter that he would never be able to repay the manning agency's fee. It didn't matter that he'd have to return home in shame, a failure. He would escape so that his life wouldn't end the way hers had.

He just had to be smart, patient, and watchful. He would look for the perfect chance to flee. Maybe it would be when they were docking at a port, maybe it would be when they were picking up new crew members. Maybe he could rely on the kindness of a stranger.

Months ago, Thiha Bo had told a story about fisherman from Cambodia who'd been rescued from another boat within the Thale fleet. A man working aboard a resupply boat had witnessed the Cambodian receiving a beating and had scraped together the money to buy out the Cambodian's contract, freeing him. Binh realized this Good Samaritan scenario was more of a dream than a plan; in fact, he suspected that the story was a fiction, something Thiha Bo had made up simply to give the rest of them hope. But a fairy tale could sustain him until he was free.

The sound of voices floated down the stairs. The two crew members tasked with making the day's meal were coming back from the kitchen, chattering about the murder. Everyone knew what had happened, even though none of them had witnessed it. The sounds of the gunfire and Mina's cries had filled the cabin below. Binh didn't want to gossip with them about it, so he turned toward the wall and squeezed his eyes tightly shut, feigning sleep. He repeated a single sentence on a loop inside his brain until a fitful sleep finally overtook him: *I will be free. I will be free*, he promised himself.

11.

EO AND SASHA had just finished a light lunch with the Kurcks and the four of them were lingering at the table, chatting, when Leo felt his phone vibrate in his pocket. He checked the display discreetly, even though there could only really be one person calling him. Hank's number appeared on the screen; Leo figured he was calling with the contact information for the Bangkok Legat. He excused himself from the table and stepped out of the dining room and onto the deck to take the call.

When he returned, Sasha and Oliver were in the middle of a spirited conversation about Singapore.

"The architecture is certainly avant-garde and cutting edge," Oliver was saying. "But a wee bit much—I mean, did you see that swimming bridge that connected the two high rises? Madness."

"I must have missed it. Connelly was excited about the restaurant scene. He even made me eat durian fruit. I just thought the entire city had such energy and vibrancy. It was invigorating," Sasha said smiling.

"Invigorating? I'll have to confess I don't share your love for Singapore, Sasha," Elli said.

Leo pocketed his phone and lowered himself back into his chair. "And why's that?" he asked, rejoining the conversation.

"I suppose it's because I find the government so oppressive," she answered slowly in a thoughtful tone of voice. "I think it's quite totalitarian and controlling about trivial matters, while real issues of disparity and injustice are disregarded and swept under the rug, as you Americans say. For instance, did you know you need a prescription to purchase chewing gum there?"

Leo laughed. "Is that really true?"

Oliver leaned across the table. "Oh, it's true all right. I learned years ago on one of our first cruises that chewing peppermint gum helps me combat my mild seasickness. For this trip, I hadn't had time to buy my gum before we left home. When we arrived in Singapore, we wasted the better part of one morning on a fool's errand trying to track down gum. It turns out that it's been banned for more than a decade, with some specific exceptions for dental gum and nicotine gum, but it's all kept under lock and key."

"I hope you were able to find something else to help with your nausea," Sasha said, giving him a concerned look.

"Oh yes, that delightful hostess procured what I needed as if by magic once we were on board. Can't say too much about the level of service and personal attention on this cruise line. Top-notch captain."

Leo was careful to avoid making eye contact with Sasha. He knew full well what she thought of their captain's personal touch.

He checked his watch. "Why don't we take a walk?" he suggested. "We have a while yet until we dock."

"I could definitely stretch my legs," Sasha agreed. Then she turned toward the Kurcks. "Care to join us?"

They stood and pushed in their chairs. Oliver draped Elli's sweater over her shoulders solicitously.

"Oh, no. You two go ahead. Elli has a massage scheduled at the spa and I'm going to take a catnap. We need to rest up for the excursion to Bangkok. I hear the tour guides maintain quite a pace once they reach the city. You may want to conserve your energy as well," Oliver suggested.

Leo smiled. "We're actually not participating in the guided excursion. We have an acquaintance in Thailand, who's graciously offered to show us around."

"How lovely," Elli murmured as she took Sasha by the shoulders and did the whole European air kiss thing on both sides of her cheeks.

"Very good," Oliver said, clapping Leo on the back.

After they said their goodbyes and the Kurcks headed toward the spa and their stateroom, respectively, Sasha and Leo strolled along the deck hand-in-hand. The usually serene ship seemed to buzz with energy as it drew nearer to the port.

"So, who's this friend of yours in Thailand?" Sasha asked.

He turned to her. "What friend?"

"The friend who's going to give us a tour of Bangkok." She gave him a look that mirrored his confusion.

He stared at her for a full thirty seconds before answering. "It's the Department of Justice attorney who Hank is setting us up with, honey."

She wrinkled her forehead. "When did you talk to Hank?"

Was she kidding? Where did she think he'd gone when he'd left the table? He pulled her over to a set of chairs and eased her down into the seat. "Are you okay?"

"I'm a little distracted," she admitted. "I keep thinking about what happened to that woman. And the kids. I'd like to talk to my parents before we disembark."

It was so rare for her to show any vulnerability, even to him, that for a moment he wasn't sure exactly how to proceed.

He spoke slowly and in a careful voice. "I know you're freaked out by what you saw, but it's important for you—for *both of us*—to stay alert. Are you telling me you really didn't notice when I got up from the table that my phone was vibrating?"

She shook her head. "I really didn't. I thought you just went to the bathroom or something. You have to admit you were pretty cagey about it. I mean, I assume that as nice as the Kurcks are, you didn't want to have a conversation with them about why you have a spy phone."

"Okay, that's a fair point. But just do me a favor. What is it Daniel always says to you about staying engaged and vigilant?" Her Krav Maga instructor was almost guaranteed to have some pithy saying appropriate for the situation.

"Keep your head on a swivel."

"Right, that. It seems like good advice for our current situation." He realized he may be overstating the potential dangers, but he wanted her to realize that they weren't in Pittsburgh anymore. The good will that came from his unofficial role with the Department of Homeland Security and her status as a local superhero attorney didn't translate into Thai. They were just two Americans in a foreign country about to stick their noses into something that didn't involve them.

He cut short his musing when she nodded her agreement then pushed herself up to standing. "Look, you don't have to worry about me being the weak link, Connelly. We're a pretty kick ass team. I've got your back."

The tightness in his chest eased at that familiar, fierce look on her face, and he smiled. "Good to know. There's no one else I'd rather go into battle with."

"You're always so romantic with your sweet nothings," she teased as she stretched up on her toes to kiss him.

12.

Laem Chabang, Thailand

J AN VAN METIER smiled, nodded, and shook hand after hand, taking care to address each passenger by name as he wished him or her a wonderful adventure in Bangkok. The vacationers streamed from the ship, overnight bags slung over their arms, headed off for their various excursions. As they filed past him, he inwardly counted the seconds until he himself would be off duty.

He had a strong need to unwind—away from the passengers, the crew members under his supervision, and the ever-watchful eye of his employer.

Most of the crew would travel the two hours to Bangkok to party or dine or otherwise blow off steam. A skeleton crew would remain on the ship to attend to the needs of those passengers who chose not to go ashore. He, however, would neither stay on the ship nor travel to Bangkok.

Instead, he would fulfill his desires at Samut Prakan, the fishing town twenty-six kilometers to the north. It was far enough away from both Laem Chabang and Bangkok that he could enjoy some measure of anonymity without worrying that he would run into an exploring passenger or a carousing crew member.

It just wouldn't do for the ship's captain to be seen indulging, even on his personal time. And Jan was always very careful to maintain an appropriate public persona; but he was, after all, still a man who needed to relax on occasion and unwind like every other human being. Today, his need to do so was perhaps greater than usual—a response to the stress of the delicate situation with that blasted Connelly woman.

Just a few more hours. He swore he could already smell the sweet, just shy of cloying, perfume that filled the smoky backroom at Bar Pavot. His anticipation mounted and his mouth began to water. He checked his watch discreetly and kept his smile frozen firmly into place.

13.

SASHA SAID GOODBYE to her parents and then to the twins, both of whom were babbling excitedly into her parents' speakerphone. Whether that excitement had anything to do with the fact that their mom and dad were cooing at them through the phone, she couldn't tell. Regardless, it was comforting to hear the sound of their laughter and to receive confirmation from her parents that Finn and Fiona hadn't completely exhausted them yet.

She handed the phone to Connelly. He made kissing noises and ended the call. He was stowing the phone in his backpack when Bruce knocked discreetly at the stateroom door. She hurried over to unlatch the door and waved him inside.

"Mrs. Connelly, Mr. Connelly. Good day." He gave a formal little nod.

"Hi, Bruce," Connelly responded cheerfully.

Bruce gave Sasha a look and tilted his head. She abandoned the overnight bag she'd been packing while on the telephone and ushered him into the small sitting room.

"I have the information you asked for, ma'am." Bruce handed her a folded piece of paper.

"Perfect. Thanks so much," she said in a low voice as she pocketed the note.

"Please don't mention it."

She suspected he meant that literally; she doubted very seriously that he had acquired what she needed without breaking at least a corporate rule or two—or maybe even a law. But, apparently, one of the great benefits of having a personal European butler of one's own was that he came, not only with impeccable manners, but with a sense of absolute loyalty, as well. It was pretty awesome, to tell the truth—even if it was just for the week.

"Understood."

He nodded and cleared his throat, speaking slightly louder than was strictly necessary as he changed the subject to include Connelly in the conversation. "Will you be staying overnight in Bangkok?"

"We will," she answered.

"Very good. Do you need a recommendation for hotel accommodations or are you all squared away?"

"Actually," Sasha said, "we have a friend here who's been gracious enough to offer to show us around and put us up."

'Friend' and 'put us up' were a slight exaggeration, but it was close enough to true. Hank had arranged for Mel Anders, the legal attaché, to pick them up and drive them to Bangkok; they'd worry about finding a hotel after they finished their business. With any luck, they'd be able to have a nice meal and a quiet night.

"What about you? Do you get the night off?" Connelly asked.

"Indeed, I do. Because you've elected to go ashore, I have a twenty-four-hour leave pass. But, as vibrant as Bangkok is, I won't be making the trip this time. I'll be visiting a nearby monastery for the evening."

"Are you a Buddhist?" Sasha asked. Now that she thought about it, Bruce's calm manner reminded her a bit of their Buddhist friend, Bodhi King.

"Not strictly, but I do find their traditions peaceful and re-centering. I like to avail myself of a quiet retreat when I can. I'm past the point in my life where I'm interested in the attractions that are so prevalent in the larger towns."

"What's Laem Chabang like?"

"Although it's small, it's a very busy city because of the port. In addition to being a port of call for several of the cruise lines, it's the country's largest port and does a bustling international shipping business. It's not as cosmopolitan as Bangkok, of course; but, it also lacks the rougher elements that the smaller fishing towns seem to attract."

Sasha saw Connelly's ears perk up at the mention of fishing towns. He walked into the sitting room to join the conversation. "So there's a lot of illegal activity in the fishing towns?"

Bruce hesitated, clearly trying to find the most polite and politic way to discuss an unsavory subject. "I'm sure that I don't know firsthand, Mr. Connelly, but my understanding is there's quite a bit of drug activity, bar fights, and perhaps some ..." he paused to clear his throat, "... prostitution. The men have a hard life out at sea, and they seem to have a need to cut loose, if you will, when they dock. I recommend avoiding any of the small fish-

ing towns on the route between here and Bangkok—Samut Prakan, in particular."

"Oh, don't worry, we'll steer clear," she assured
him with a smile.

"Is there anything else I can get for you before
you disembark? Perhaps some bottles of mineral
water to take along for the drive? Or a first aid kit
or snacks?" He slipped seamlessly back into his valet role.

She patted her overstuffed tote bag. "I think
we're covered. I'm pretty much a pro at packing a
diaper bag for twins. If I don't have it in here, we
likely don't need it."

"Very good. Enjoy your trip. Will you need a
porter to carry your bags?"

"Nope. We've got it," Connelly said.

At that, Bruce nodded and left the suite. Connelly waited until they heard Bruce shut the outer
door behind him, then he said, "Mind telling me
what that was all about?"

She grinned at him. "I thought we should try to
give this legal attaché guy something more helpful
to go on than 'some fishing boat in the Gulf of
Thailand.'"

He gave her a careful look. "Unfortunately, that's
the extent of our knowledge."

"That *was* the extent of our knowledge. But I may have led Bruce to believe that I have a corporate client interested in acquiring a fleet of fishing boats that would operate out of this area," she began, enjoying the growing look of amazement on her husband's face as she spoke.

"Did you really?"

"I really did. I explained that I was just beginning to research the industry and it would be extremely useful to know which were the biggest fleets that operate in the Gulf of Thailand. I told him I was especially interested in fleets that currently have boats out there right now and asked if he could help me out, stressing the importance of confidentiality." She waved the paper at him. "And our man Bruce came through. It's a starting point, at least."

"You continually amaze me."

She recognized both his tone of voice and the look he was giving her. "Well, I'm glad to hear I've still got it, but we don't have time for what you have in mind."

Connelly checked his watch then hooked his thumb under the strap of her tote bag and slid it off her shoulder. "I beg to differ," he half-purred, half-growled.

14.

MEL ANDERS TURNED out to be a tall, brown-eyed blonde with short curly hair that corkscrewed out from her head in every direction, like springs. She spotted them the moment they stepped out onto the dock and strode toward them, elbows pumping. "Sasha? Leo?" she asked, her hand already outstretched. Sasha took it first; the woman's grip was firm and brisk.

"You must be Mel," Connelly said.

She nodded. "Right. I'll bet you were expecting a guy."

"Well, actually, I was," he confessed.

"I get that a lot. But I find it easier to go by my childhood nickname. It just ... simplifies things."

Sasha could only imagine that the old boys' club so alive and well in the West was at least equally robust in Asia.

"I'm sure. Is Mel short for Melissa? Melanie?" she asked.

Mel gave her a wry look. "Melody. My mom had this dream that I would become a singer. Melody was shortened to Mel pretty quickly once it became clear that I can't carry a tune in a bucket." She laughed a raspy laugh then waved them toward her car. "We should probably get going. It's a long drive."

"We really appreciate your meeting us like this," Connelly said as he folded himself into the back of the dark, nondescript sedan. Apparently, Sasha reflected as she slid into the front passenger seat, government-issued cars were the same the world over.

"Don't mention it. I don't know Agent Richardson, other than by reputation, but my boss has been on assignment with him several times and says he's a stand-up guy. And Ron gave me clear marching orders: Any friend of Hank's is a friend of ours." In one quick gesture, the legal attaché fastened her seatbelt, gunned the car, and peeled out into a flow of traffic that, as far as Sasha could tell, followed no discernible pattern.

Sasha discretely tugged on her own seatbelt to confirm that it was locked into place. The motion didn't escape Mel's notice, and she laughed again. "You'll get used to the driving around here."

"How long have you been stationed here?" Connelly asked.

She tapped her light pink fingernails on the steering wheel as she thought, "I started out in the Tokyo office, but I've been here almost a year now. I like Thailand. It has a different feel."

Connelly leaned forward from the back seat. "How did you end up assigned to the Southeast Asian division in the first place? Were you an Asian Studies major?"

Mel shook her head. "I was a math major, if you can believe it. I specialized in a kind of theoretical math called category math. I figured I'd end up a professor somewhere. But, in my junior year, a teaching assistant for one of my elective courses caught my eye. He was a Chinese national. We've been married for three years now. When things got serious between us, I decided to learn Chinese so I could talk to his family and found out I have an ear for languages."

Sasha glanced over at her. "How many do you speak?"

She let go of the steering wheel and ticked them off on her fingers. "Let's see, I picked up Mandarin and Japanese pretty quickly. My Thai's not bad; and I can also speak Malay and Vietnamese. I just started studying Burmese. Anyway, once I mastered a few foreign languages, I decided that seeing the world might be a little more fun than seeing the inside of a college lecture hall every day. So, instead of signing up for the GRE exam, I wandered into career services and signed up for interviews with the Foreign Service and the Bureau. The FBI hired me."

She met Connelly's eyes in the rearview mirror. "I started out in D.C., and as you know, the Legat Service usually chooses pretty seasoned agents to serve overseas. But I got lucky because my language skills impressed the Tokyo Legat; he pulled all sorts of strings to get me assigned as his ALAT. And the rest, as they say, is history."

"ALAT?" Sasha echoed.

"Assistant Legal Attaché."

They drove in silence for a moment or two. Mel whizzed by scooters, open-air buses, and cars, weaving in and out of the flow of traffic with expert timing. There didn't appear to be set lanes. Sasha focused on taking long, slow breaths and pushed aside visions of dying in a fiery multi-vehicle crash.

"The traffic will die down as soon as we're outside the city," Mel assured her. "Of course, then the road goes to pot. But at least it won't be so congested—it won't pick back up again until we get to the next port town." She laughed.

Sasha managed a weak smile. "Did Hank explain to your legat why we need your help?"

"All Ron told me was that you believe you witnessed some sort of crime in the Gulf. You immediately reported it to the captain of your cruise ship, who took no action."

"That's right as far as it goes," Connelly confirmed.

Sasha cut to the chase. "I saw the murder of a woman on a fishing boat. She was shot multiple times and her body either fell or was pushed into the ocean."

Mel's eyes widened but she kept her attention on the road. She was silent for a moment then said, "You sound pretty sure."

"I am."

"Here's the thing. Women don't typically go out on the trawlers. In fact, I don't think I've ever seen a female on a fishing vessel."

"I know what I saw."

Mel chewed on her lower lip. "I don't suppose you were close enough to see any details—the boat's number or flag or anything?"

"No."

"Sasha did some poking around," Connelly said. "Go ahead, tell her."

"I asked a ... um ... source for a list of the biggest companies that routinely fish in the Gulf of Thailand and their countries of registry." She removed Bruce's list from her handbag and unfolded it. "He was kind enough to star the ones that are known to be out at sea in this area right now. It looks like there are only two—Indonesia Fishery, Inc. and Thale Company."

Mel arched a perfectly shaped brow but didn't press her on the source. "That sounds right. Most of the big trawlers tend to go out further where there's less competition. The little guys stay closer to land. Why do you think it's a big outfit?"

"The guns, mainly. I think the shooters were hired help. I assume a village fisherman with a single boat wouldn't have that kind of firepower on retainer."

"That's probably right," Mel said in a thoughtful voice. "Indonesia Fishery runs a pretty clean operation."

"But Thale doesn't?" Connelly asked.

"I wouldn't say that. But let's just say the family that runs Thale is something of an empire; they have a hand in pretty much every local industry. They're very powerful and well-connected politically. Wealthy."

"Meaning they know who to bribe?" Sasha guessed.

"Sure. They usually skirt the line—right up to the edge of legality—but when they do get into trouble, it gets taken care of. But that hardly makes them unique. Corruption is part of the culture."

"That must make your job challenging."

Mel nodded. "You could say that. It took some getting used to. Let me tell you, though, it's nothing like Korea ..." She trailed off, shaking her head.

"Could you see Thale commissioning a murder?" Connelly asked.

"I don't know."

"Their fleet is registered out of Cambodia," Sasha noted. "Indonesia Fisheries boats are registered out of Indonesia."

Mel grimaced. "Most of my work is on land, but the maritime industry here is significant enough that even I know Cambodia's a problem."

"A problem how?"

"It's a notorious flag of convenience country. Cambodia runs an open registry, no questions asked. Cambodia-flagged ships have been implicated in everything from illegal smuggling to safety violations to you name it. The country cashes the checks and turns a blind eye."

"What's our first move? It sounds like reporting Thale to the Cambodian authorities would be futile. Would Thai law enforcement be willing to investigate?" Sasha asked.

It seemed reasonably clear that Thailand would have the legal authority to prosecute a Thai company. But she'd had enough interactions with the criminal justice system to know that jurisdiction and motivation were two separate animals.

Mel shrugged. "I'm not sure, honestly. We need to get you to the embassy and sit down with Ron. He'll know the political situation better than I do."

~ ~ ~ ~ ~ ~ ~ ~ ~ ~ ~

While Sasha and the assistant legal attaché discussed whether the United Nations' International Maritime Organization might be the appropriate agency to handle the murder inquiry, Leo shifted his attention to the countryside outside the window. The condition of the road had deteriorated almost instantly once they were outside the city limits, and he bounced slightly on the backseat as the car bounced along. The road twisted along the sapphire water's edge. Birds, trees, and waves made up most of the view. Every so often, a weathered road sign would appear, hammered into the strip of grass that separated the road from the beach. He couldn't read the lettering, but based on the numbers, he assumed they were announcing the distances to Bangkok and interim points of interest.

His stomach rumbled, and he waited for a pause so that he could inject himself into the conversation.

"Are we getting close to a town?" he asked.

In the rearview mirror, he could see Mel's brown eyes narrow in response to the question. "Pretty close. Why?"

"Why don't we stop for a quick bite and a rest? I know Ron's made a reservation for dinner tonight but I also know the Bureau well enough that once we sit down and start talking about murder, that reservation's going to get pushed back, then pushed back again, and then finally cancelled. And I'm not interested in eating microwaved ramen noodles out of a Styrofoam cup while we're all hunched around a conference room table. Are you?"

With a tilt of her head, Mel conceded that he had drawn a fairly accurate description of her working dinners. He wasn't surprised. U.S. Embassy in Bangkok, Department of Justice headquarters, or the Academy in Quantico—the Bureau was the Bureau was the Bureau.

She nodded her head. "Not really. But this next town is a bit sketchy."

Sasha piped up, "I'm not really hungry. Why don't we push on? I'd like to get the 'doing our duty as good citizens' portion of this vacation behind us and return to the 'enjoying cocktails and sunsets' portion."

"Duly noted. But I'm starving." Then he moved in for the kill, "And I'm sure the coffee's abysmal at Mel's office."

Mel snorted. "It's drinkable in the morning, but the Embassy is full of tea drinkers. By mid-afternoon, the only available coffee is the burnt, warmed-over mud left in the bottom of the pot."

Sasha jerked her head back as if she'd been slapped. "*Tea*? Well, I guess a quick stop for a snack for you two and a cup of decent coffee for me wouldn't hurt. Do you need to call Ron and run it by him?"

Mel, whose face said clearly that she did, waved away the notion with one hand. "No need to bother him. We'll be quick."

"Is it safe to stop? You just said it's a tough town."

"It's no worse than any East Coast city in the States. As long as we stay out of the neighborhoods near the piers we should be fine," Mel assured her.

15.

AN FORCED HIMSELF to slow his stride as he neared the front door of the bar. It would be unseemly to appear eager or enthusiastic, as if he *needed* to visit. He held himself to strict rules and limitations regarding his indulgences. In his view, it was the only responsible way to fulfill his professional duties and satisfy his appetite. A girl in a bar in Hong Kong had told him there was a name for someone like him—a 'chipper.' Chipper sounded much better than the alternatives—junkie, user, doper, all unsavory names for unsavory characters.

He pushed open the red door and walked inside the dimly lit bar. He hesitated in the doorway until his eyes adjusted to the darkness. Then he continued through the small dining room in the front, past the raucous bar, already half-full with men from the fisheries and women from heavens-only-knew-where, and through a narrow corridor. Behind the restrooms, he hung a left and walked to the end of the hall. He stopped in front of a door that seemed almost deliberately nondescript. Plain light wood. No sign. No indication of what lay behind it.

He raised his fist and rapped twice on the wood. He cleared his throat and clasped his hands together behind his back to still their anticipatory trembling.

Muffled footsteps sounded on the other side of the door. A moment later, the door cracked open. Jan recognized the burly Thai who peered out at him but couldn't match a name to the scarred face.

The man stared at him impassively, waiting.

"I have a reservation," Jan said in a voice that cracked ever so slightly.

The Thai nodded then looked him over from head to toe. "No kit?"

"No. I prefer to smoke. The cigarettes," he specified lest the man try to hand him a glass pipe. Only an addict would use a pipe or, even worse, inject himself with heroin. And sliding a tube around on a piece of aluminum foil was undignified. A nice, hand-rolled cigarette suited him just fine.

Another curt nod, then the door opened wider, and Jan stepped inside.

16.

MEL LED SASHA and Connelly along a narrow street until they reached a chic-looking building. The façade was painted a glossy black and the front door was bright red. A sign overhead read 'Bar Pavot' in curly lettering in English with the Thai script below.

"This is it," Mel announced.

"It looks pretty nice." Sasha couldn't hide her surprise. Given Bruce and Mel's warnings about the fishing towns, she'd expected something much grittier.

"The town's going through a transition. It's still very rough around the edges but the tourism industry is picking up. This place is one of the newer, more upscale bistros. It caters to a foreign crowd even though I believe it's locally owned," Mel explained.

"'Pavot' is French isn't it? Some kind of flower, I think," Sasha mused, half to herself.

Connelly snorted. "You aren't going to pretend that you speak French again, are you?"

She rolled her eyes. "I explained this to you when we were in Quebec City. I took French literature. I can *read* French, not speak it."

Connelly turned to Mel. "And by 'read it,' she means she can read poems and stuff by dead guys like Balzac and Baudelaire. She *doesn't* mean she can read anything useful like a map or a restaurant menu—just so we're clear." He pulled Sasha in a half-hug to lessen the sting of his needling.

Mel laughed. "I think it means 'poppy.' Anyway, they serve good French coffee and a great meat and cheese board. Something for everyone." She pushed open the door, and they stepped inside.

A smiling hostess in a black-and-white striped dress whisked them to a window seat in the cozy dining room in the front of the bistro. As they settled into their seats, Connelly and Mel studied the menu, and Sasha studied her surroundings. The bar, which was located behind the dining room, was rocking. Laughter and loud voices rose over the sound of live music.

"Are you sure you just want coffee, Sasha?" Mel asked.

She turned her attention back to the table and scanned the menu for a moment. "Are we really going to miss dinner?"

"It's a definite possibility," Mel admitted. "Ron's going to want to get a very thorough statement from you given that you'll be leaving the country tomorrow night."

Sasha sighed. "I guess I'll have the mussels."

"Well, if we're all eating, we might as well get a bottle of wine. It's what the French would do, you know," Mel said.

"I don't think we need a whole bottle. Let's just each get a glass," Connelly suggested.

Mel's expression grew serious and she leaned forward. "Okay, listen up. This is an important safety tip. While you're in here, do not—I repeat, do not—drink anything in any bar or restaurant that doesn't arrive at your table in a sealed container."

"Wow. Really?"

"Really. There have been instances where tourists' drinks have been spiked with everything from LSD to Rohypnol to Lord knows what. The idea is to render the mark incapacitated and then rob them or worse. Even in a nicer place like this it's best to be cautious," Mel said matter-of-factly.

"Thanks for the warning," Connelly said. He perused the wine list. "Hmm, a merlot or a cabernet sauvignon?"

Sasha had a more pressing concern. "Wait, then how am I supposed to get my coffee?"

"Oh, no worries. This place serves a great bottled coffee."

Sasha narrowed her eyes. *"Bottled coffee?"* This news was easily as troubling as the risk of being drugged.

"You'll love it," Mel promised. "It's a dark cold-brewed coffee they order directly from a roaster in Bangkok."

Sasha made a noncommittal noise. "We'll see."

Just then, a waiter materialized to take their order. Sasha took a deep breath and ordered the bottled coffee.

The food and drinks arrived quickly, and as they ate, they chatted—mainly about Mel's experiences as an American woman living and working in Southeast Asia. She was quick-witted and funny, and the time passed quickly. Sasha almost forgot that this wasn't a social visit, and Mel wasn't an old friend. She was an authorized representative of the United States government who was trying to help them ensure that a murdered woman received some measure of justice.

With that sobering thought, Sasha looked up and met Connelly's eyes over the table. He was staring past her—his gaze locked on something or someone over her right shoulder. She twisted in her seat to see what had caught his attention.

"What is it?" Sasha asked.

Connelly held up a finger as he cocked his head to listen intently. After a moment, he said, "A couple of guys at the bar are griping, in English, about Thale. I guess they had a ship come in today unexpectedly. The name caught my ear."

Mel nodded. "That's not really surprising. Like I said, this is a big fishing town. And Thale's a big fishing company. If memory serves, it has its own pier down at the docks."

Sasha blinked at her. "So the ship that docked— it could be the one I saw."

"It could be. The odds are against it, though. Thale has an entire fleet," Mel pointed out.

"Sure, but if the boat that came in today wasn't scheduled to be here, that means something out of the ordinary happened. It doesn't *have* to mean that extraordinary event was a murder ... but it seems to me that fact changes the odds somewhat."

The legat shrugged. "Maybe."

Sasha wasn't a big believer in coincidences. "Connelly, what do you think?"

"It might be nothing—could just be a ship that needs a repair or has run out of some important supply and can't wait for the resupply boat to come out. Or it might be something—a captain running scared because a girl was shot to death and now he has a panicked crew. I don't know." He rested his forearms on the table, leaned in close, and lowered his voice to a near-whisper, "But I know an easy way to find out."

"How's that?" Mel asked in a voice tinged with suspicion.

"You two wait here. I'll take a walk down to the docks and poke around."

"No way," Mel answered.

"Absolutely not," Sasha added.

"Sasha—" Connolly began.

She cut him off. "Don't Sasha me. You are not going to go skulking around the docks alone in some violent, crime-infested Thai village."

She watched as he stiffened.

"Do I really need to remind you that I'm a veteran federal agent? You know I *do* know how to handle myself."

Mel was suddenly transfixed by the pattern on the tablecloth. Apparently, wading into a marital dispute was above her pay grade.

"I'm not saying you don't. I'm saying you're not going without me. It'll be—"

It was his turn to cut her off. "Please tell me you weren't about to say 'fun.' This isn't some sort of cloak-and-dagger game. You saw a woman murdered. We have two children to think about. And you aren't trained to do this. I am."

They locked eyes. After about ten seconds, Sasha realized that he was right, but she wasn't about to give in that easily. So she continued to eyeball him, staring hard, hoping Mel would chime in soon.

After a moment, the legal attaché cleared her throat. "What's your plan? You're just going to stroll down to the docks and make them talk? These guys at the bar may speak some English, but the men actually working on the boats ... I'm not so sure."

"Why not? If this is such a hard-scrabble town, good old American currency should be able to inspire some dockworkers to give up what they know about Thale. I've found that cash can bridge a lot of language barriers."

"Well, bribery *is* a time-honored tradition around here," Mel conceded.

Sasha jumped in. "Why don't all three of us go? Then I'll be one hapless civilian in the company of two seasoned federal agents. I'd be completely safe. And Mel can translate for you."

He shook his head. "Look, I'm half-Vietnamese, so I have some chance of blending in down there if I go alone. But if I stroll up with a tall blonde and a tiny green-eyed American, I'll stand out like ... a kitten in a dog show."

She couldn't resist laughing at his tortured simile, but her smile faded quickly. "Mel, you aren't going to go along with this are you?"

Mel's expression was pained. "I shouldn't. Ron will be apoplectic when he hears about it. But ... if the boat *is* down there now, we should find out so we can stop it before it goes back out to sea. It could be gone for months. And the jurisdiction gets way messier if we try to board it on the open sea. This could be a real opportunity."

Sasha opened her mouth but Mel steamrolled along. "I don't love the idea of him going down there alone, but the reality is, he's right. You and I would stick out and draw attention. It's broad daylight, and he's a big guy. I don't think anyone will mess with him." She checked her watch then turned to Connelly. "Just be smart about it. Find out if it's the boat that was in the gulf earlier and then get the hell out of there. No heroics. Meet us back at the car in, say, thirty minutes."

"Will do."

While Mel sketched a quick map to the private docks on her napkin, Connelly bent and kissed Sasha just above the ear.

"I'll be careful," he promised.

"I know you will, but that doesn't mean I have to like it."

"Welcome to my world," he smirked.

17.

JAN WAS UNBELIEVABLY comfortable and warm, enveloped in the embrace of the heroin. He'd been suspended in a half-awake, half-asleep dream state for some time. How long exactly, he couldn't say. Although the rest of his life ran on a timetable with military precision, when he was in the den, smoking, he lost all track of time.

That wasn't quite true. It was more that time began to bend and undulate, whirling around him like the smoke---circular, not linear, and ephemeral, utterly without import. He relished this languid feeling.

But bodily functions could only be ignored for so long. And Jan needed to use the head. He reluctantly forced himself up from the deep, plush couch. His arms and legs felt as heavy as his eyelids as he made his way to the door. He stumbled out into the hallway with the laughter of the door-man/heroin dealer floating behind.

After using the facilities and washing his hands, he felt more alert and suddenly hungry. He splashed cold water on face and straightened his shirt then headed to the bar to place an order. He intended to hole up at Bar Pavot for the duration of his shore time, eating, and sleeping, and smoking. Cherise, the smiling Chinese waitress assigned to the bar today, took his order and promised to bring the sandwich and a bottle of water back to him in the private room. He thanked her and turned to leave.

As his pivoted away from the bar, he heard loud female laughter rising over the music. It was com-ing from the dining room. The sound caught his attention even through the fog that was still settled over his brain. As a rule, he'd always found Asian women to be less boisterous, more demure than their Western counterparts. Curious, he glanced toward the source of the laughter.

Two women—one blonde, who sat facing the bar, and one brunette, with her back to the bar. Both obviously Westerners and, if he were to hazard a guess, both American. He frowned. The women were unaccompanied by men and, in his view, were foolish to draw so much attention to themselves. Bar Pavot was one of the nicer establishments in town, but they were still in Samut Prakan, after all.

Well, their safety was not his concern. His concern waited for him, rolled tightly in a cigarette.

And yet. He couldn't stop staring at the women. An anxious pocket of his brain was fighting through his heroin-induced chill to worry that they might be cruise passengers or crew members, liable to expose his secret if they bumped into him here. He narrowed his eyes and stepped closer to the low dividing wall that separated the dining area from the bar area.

No, he didn't recognize the blonde. She was neither a crew member nor a passenger. The brunette, however, *was* a passenger. And, he realized, as she turned her head and he saw her profile, not just any passenger. It was Sasha McCandless-Connelly. His initial anxiety gave way to irritation and flaring anger. How dare she, the cause of so much of his current stress, show up *here*.

As he stood staring at the two women, a waiter juggling a large, round tray jostled him, and he hurriedly moved aside. Where was the Connelly woman's husband? And who was the blonde woman? He was certain she wasn't one of the passengers. He prided himself on matching every name on the manifest to a face within the first day of every cruise.

He considered their attire. Although Sasha Connelly wore standard garb for a woman on holiday—a sundress, sandals, and a light sweater—the other woman wore a dark, no-nonsense business suit. He searched the recesses of his memory. Mrs. Connelly was, if he recalled correctly, an attorney. He supposed she might have a colleague or an old law school chum living in Thailand. But Samut Prakan was not the sort of place where people like Sasha Connelly tended to spend their free time.

That was the entire point. He chose the port town for his personal recreational activities because his passengers would not be there. *Why were they here?*

The band finished its set and announced a break. The noise level fell in the bar and, if he strained forward, he could just hear a snippet of their conversation. What he heard chilled him and chased away the lingering remnants of euphoria.

He distinctly heard the words 'embassy' and 'girl's murder' from the Connelly woman.

As he watched, the blonde woman nodded, her face grave. He focused on the movement of her lips and strained to hear her response. 'The Bureau ... Bangkok police ... the IMO ... murder.' The disjointed words that floated back to him over the noise seemed to be intended to reassure Sasha Connelly, but they struck Jan in the face with the force of their meaning.

Jan saw the Connelly woman relax her shoulders. Then the blonde met his eyes and wrinkled her forehead. He realized he was staring. The blonde woman half-rose from her seat, and Mrs. Connelly twisted around to get a look at him. Jan turned on his heel and pushed through the bar crowd. He raced down the hall to the back room and pounded on the door in a panic until it opened.

Before the bouncer could growl at him about causing a commotion, Jan grabbed him by the shoulders. "You need to call your boss. Now."

18.

L EO WALKED PURPOSEFULLY toward the
dock but didn't hurry. He didn't want anyone
who might be watching him to sense urgency
or fear. He whistled. He was pleasantly surprised
he'd been able to convince Sasha and Mel to go
along with his plan.

All he needed to do was eyeball the boats, confirm whether the Thale vessel was, in fact, docked,
and find a dockworker who spoke adequate English
and who was willing to confirm that there'd been a
woman aboard. A few minutes of legwork, and he'd
be able to help Mel and her boss build a case
against Thale; more importantly, he and Sasha
would be able to put this mess behind them and

return to their regularly scheduled program of cocktails and sunsets.

As he got closer to the sea, the neighborhood changed rapidly. The tourist-friendly veneer slipped away, replaced by crowded streets strewn with litter and rodents. Broken glass cracked under his feet as he walked. The storefronts gave way to dilapidated shanties and boarded-up shacks. The pungent smell of fish permeated the air.

He passed a row of large, metal containers lined up, probably waiting to be filled with the day's catch. A handful of boats were tied to the rotting, wooden dock. Each looked more battered and un-seaworthy than the next. The numerals and characters that identified the vessels were uniformly faded, obscured, or missing entirely. Leo figured that was likely by design.

Voices shouting directions near the boat at the far end of the pier caught his attention and he walked toward the sound. A crew of men was engaged in a whirlwind of activity, hauling buckets and containers from the deck of the ship onto the dock in an assembly line. He approached the man closest to him, who handed the buckets off to a runner—a lithe teenaged boy, who raced across the dock to a refrigerated container, where he emptied each bucket and then ran back for another.

Leo waited until the boy took off toward the containers.

"English? Do you speak English?" he asked the man.

The man raised his weathered, lined face and looked at Leo with tired, bloodshot eyes. He shook his head no, rested the bucket on the ground for a moment, and jerked his thumb toward a round-faced, smiling man in the middle of the line. "Thiha Bo. English," he said in labored, heavily accented English.

Leo bowed his head in gratitude then pressed a few crumpled bills into the man's free hand. "Thank you."

The tired eyes widened in shock at the sight of American currency. He stuffed the bills in his pocket before anyone else could notice and grabbed the next bucket as the runner returned.

Leo approached the fisherman who had been identified as an English speaker. He was in a state of constant, rapid motion, reaching back to grab a bucket and flinging it forward to the next man in the chain without pause. Leo waited. After several moments, there was a break in the action.

He stepped forward. "Thiha Bo?"

The man nodded. "*Hotekae.*"

"You speak English?" Leo enunciated and spoke slowly.

A shadow of suspicion flitted across the man's face, but he nodded again. "*Hotekae*, yes. I speak English." His pronunciation had a British lilt.

"My name is Leo Nguyen." It stung to use his father's surname rather than his own, but he was certain it was the right choice under the circumstances. "I'm looking for a girl."

Thiha Bo erupted with guttural laugh. "You're in the wrong place, Leo Nguyen. The girls are in the bars. Or look for a red light."

Leo shook his head. "Not that kind of girl. A girl who works on a fishing boat." He watched the man's reaction closely.

The leer gave way to a look of wide-eyed astonishment, which morphed almost instantly into an expression of fear. He took his time responding. "Men only are permitted on the boats."

Leo took a step closer and lowered his voice. "What happened to her?"

Thiha Bo clamped his mouth shut and looked away. His smile vanished and his lips were set in a thin line. The line resumed its work, and the man focused on passing the buckets.

Leo considered pushing him further, but Thiha Bo's reaction had given him the answer he needed.

This was the right boat. He reached into his pocket for more cash, but when he tried to hand the money to Thiha Bo, the fisherman refused it.

"Please, take it. It's a gesture of my thanks."

"No. It is not necessary, Leo Nguyen. I was not able to help you find your girl."

Leo hesitated. He didn't want to argue with the man and draw attention to them. "Please, Thiha Bo. I insist."

The man relented and took the money with a little bow. Leo turned and walked away. He'd gone about four feet when Thiha Bo called after him, "Leo Nguyen!"

Leo turned. Thiha Bo abandoned his spot in the line and jogged over to where he stood. "I will take you to see Binh. He knows about the girl."

19.

SASHA TURNED AROUND to get a look at the pervert Mel said was staring at them, but no one was standing between the bar and the dining room. "Where'd he go?"

"He took off. I'm sure it was nothing. He was just a garden-variety barfly," Mel assured her.

But Mel herself didn't seem quite convinced of that. The legal attaché's face was pale and drawn.

"Are you sure? You look pretty shaken up," Sasha told her.

Mel picked up her wineglass and took a sip before responding. "I mean, yeah, he creeped me out. I'm not sure why, to tell you the truth. He looked really very normal. He was a Caucasian dude. Older. Buttoned up. Not the sort of guy you'd expect to give you trouble. But the way he was looking at us.... He had this dazed expression, like he was half out of it, but he was staring at us so hard. It just ..." She gave a little shudder and trailed off.

Sasha sipped her wine as well. Social convention would say they should just shake off the unsettling incident. But social convention was no friend to women. Krav Maga had taught her not to ignore her instincts out of some warped desire to be seen as polite or nice or feminine.

They sat in silence for a moment. The noise from the bar, no longer masked by the live music of the band, sounded somehow more threatening and ominous. Less like a rowdy celebration and more like a riot about to boil over. Sasha knew Mel could feel the difference, too, because her eyes kept flitting over Sasha's shoulder to the raucous crowd behind them.

Enough of this.

Sasha pushed her wineglass away and chugged the rest of the bottled coffee. She returned the empty bottle to the table with a dull thud. "Why don't we pay our check and walk down to the car. We can wait for Connelly there," she suggested. She deliberately kept her voice light.

Mel, who clearly shared her sense of unease, wasn't fooled by her tone. She agreed instantly. "Great idea." She nodded her head and signaled for the waiter to bring their check.

Apparently the waiter missed the signal. Several moments passed in excruciating slowness before he wandered by again. Sasha stretched out her arm and tugged on his sleeve. "Can we get our check, please?"

"Oh, you ladies shouldn't go running off so soon. The night's just getting started." He smiled broadly at both of them.

"We have an important appointment in Bangkok. We need our check right away so we're not late," Mel said, her voice all business.

The waiter lowered his eyes and nodded. "Ah, our loss is Bangkok's gain, eh? I'll be right back." He walked to the back of the room and turned to give them a long look before disappearing into a dimly lit hallway behind the bar.

"Isn't the cash register in the front near the hostess station?" Sasha asked, her eyes still on the hallway. She tried, without success, to shake the feeling of foreboding that had settled over her.

Mel didn't answer. She pulled out her phone and unlocked the screen. "I'm just going to send Ron a message and give him our ETA."

It was a completely ordinary, natural thing to do—to let your boss know when to expect you back. And yet, Sasha got the distinct impression that Mel's message was intended to provide a time-line of events in case someone ever needed it later.

Goosebumps rose on Sasha's arms and she pulled her light cotton sweater tighter around her shoulders. She scanned the hallway again, but there was no sign of their waiter. "How much do you think the bill came to?" She opened her purse and took out a fistful of Thai currency. "Will this cover it?"

Mel glanced at the bills fanned out in Sasha's hand and laughed. "That would more than cover it. Not to mention a very generous tip. But let me get this; I'll put it on the corporate card and get reimbursed."

Sasha could hear shakiness in her voice when she answered. "No, listen. I've got a bad feeling. I want to get out of here. I'm skeeved out by the fact that some guy was watching us. Our waiter gave me a weird vibe and now he's taking a really long time. Let's just go back to the car."

Mel looked as though she was about to argue, but just then the sound of glass crashing and male voices raised in testosterone-laced anger rose from the bar and filled the space. She stood and pushed back her chair. "Yeah, I'd say that's our cue to go."

Sasha threw the money on the table, and they hurried out of the restaurant.

~ ~ ~ ~ ~ ~ ~ ~ ~ ~

Jan was in the sweet embrace of another cigarette, his eyes rolled back into his head, as he floated in that space between wakefulness and asleep. Suddenly, a flurry of knocks rained down on the wooden door, as if someone was pounding with both fists. He tried to focus and push himself up from the couch, but his head lolled back against the cushion. He giggled.

The doorman let out an exasperated grunt as he walked across the room and yanked the door open. One of the waiters stood in the doorway, yammering in rapid-fire Thai. Whatever he was going on about had him all in a lather, and Jan thought that his excited hand gestures resembled the flapping wings of a bird. After another brief back and forth, the drug dealer barked out a few words of dismissal and waved the waiter back into the restaurant. He closed the door and turned toward Jan. His face was a mask of anger and frustration.

"What's wrong?" Jan managed to say through his near-stupor.

The giant of a man rubbed his hand over his bald head, thinking, before he responded. "Your American friends left. The boss told me to have their waiter stall them until he could get a team here. But now they're gone and it's on my head."

The Americans? Oh, right, Sasha McCandless-Connelly and her friend from the Embassy.

He noted the man's tense, set jaw. "You look up-tight. Here, have a smoke. My treat." He extended the rosewood box that held the bundle of heroin cigarettes he'd purchased from the Thai earlier in the day.

The man waved it away in disgust. "Keep your junk away from me. I need to think clearly. I have to clean up this mess."

"Suit yourself, friend." Jan leaned back, unoffended, and watched with amusement as the man paced a tight line back and forth across the small room.

His muscles bunched up in his back and neck, creating bulges in his suit. After several trips across the room, muttering under his breath, he swung the combination lock to open the wall safe in the corner and reached inside. He removed a set of keys, a bundle of cash, and a snub-nosed gun. Jan started to ask where he was going, but halfway through the question, he nodded off.

The sound of the door slamming barely registered in his dream.

20.

HIHA BO LED Leo to the boat. He gestured with his hand for Leo to stay back, partially hidden behind a barrel. When the time was right, he waved for Leo to follow him, and they crept up a rickety makeshift ramp. The board splintered and split as Leo ascended it. He froze and held his breath for a moment, waiting to see if it would yield completely and cleave in half under his weight. The board groaned but somehow held.

The stench on the deck stung his eyes and burned his lungs. It wasn't merely the smell of fish. It was something foul and dank, festering. It smelled like sickness or like a room that hadn't been cleaned in too long. Even the breeze blowing across the water didn't clear the scent. It hung heavy like a cloud over everything. He coughed and buried his nose in his sleeve.

Thiha Bo turned and frowned, raising a cautionary finger to his lips.

Leo nodded. 'Sorry,' he mouthed.

They sneaked further toward the front of the dilapidated boat. The fisherman stole quietly on his bare feet. Leo cursed his heavy leather shoes.

The deck seemed to be deserted, the crew all busy on the pier unloading their haul. But there was no guarantee that there weren't people below deck. Evidently, this Binh person was on the boat. How many others were there?

Unanswered questions pricked at him. If he'd known they were going to board the vessel, he'd have demanded the pertinent information: how many people; where were they located; whether they were inclined to look the other way, sound an alarm, or rush him. He glanced over the edge at the dirty water. He knew his most likely emergency escape route, at least. Right over the side.

When they had nearly reached the bow, Thiha Bo veered to the right and led him to a small cabin.

"Captain's private quarters," he whispered, gesturing toward the cheap plywood door.

Thiha Bo smiled, but Leo stiffened. He was putting a great deal of trust into a stranger—too much trust, he knew. But he didn't have a lot of options. And the Burmese man didn't set off any warning bells in his brain.

Still, he kept a close watch on his guide—ready to tackle him or use him as a shield as the situation warranted—as the man eased the door open. *The door wasn't locked?* A frisson of shock ran along his spine as he crossed the threshold into the dark room. Once his eyes adjusted to the dim light, his surprise evaporated. After all, what need was there to lock the door when the cargo inside was secured?

Three large, rectangular wire cages lined the far wall. Leo judged them to be about four feet high by two-and-a-half feet wide. Two of the cages were empty. The third held a kneeling man, his hands bound in front of him with thick fishing rope. He raised his eyes fearfully and tensed when they entered the room, but when he recognized Thiha Bo, his shoulders relaxed. His face remained watchful and guarded.

Thiha Bo crossed the room and squatted in front of the cage. He spoke to the man inside in a low, soothing tone. It took Leo a moment to realize he was speaking Vietnamese. He didn't know enough of his father's language to follow the conversation but he could pick out isolated words and phrases. One word caught his attention: *con gái*, daughter. He'd learned the words for family relations before he'd traveled as a teenager to Vietnam to search for his father. The word filled him with dread. If Thiha Bo thought he might be the dead woman's father, that meant she had been very young—at most, a teenager.

The man in the cage hung his head sorrowfully for a moment. When he raised his face to Leo, tears shined in his eyes. "You were Mina's father?" he asked in Vietnamese.

Mina. Now at least she had a name.

Leo shook his head no and looked to Thiha Bo. "Please tell him I'm not her father. I'm ... a friend. Someone who wants to help," he said in English.

Thiha Bo translated the message. Binh started to shake his head wildly from side to side then choked out a response that Leo didn't understand.

"He says it's too late to help her. He says to tell you he's very sorry to say that your friend is dead." Thiha Bo's voice was mournful.

"Why is he caged?"

"Binh knew she was a girl and kept her secret. When the soldiers killed her, he tried not to react. But his soul reacted. Someone heard him weeping in his hammock and told the captain. This is his punishment for insubordination."

The explanation raised more questions than Leo could possibly ask. So he settled for asking the most pressing first. "Did you say soldiers killed her?"

Thiha Bo frowned. "Not government soldiers. Private soldiers. I'm sorry, I don't know the word in your language."

Leo did. *Mercenaries. Contractors. Paid killers.*

"Why would someone tell the captain that Binh cared about the girl?"

"Currying favor," Thiha Bo explained. "Captain Vũ, he doesn't like the Vietnamese. If you get one in trouble, you get better treatment. Extra food. Easier work." He shrugged.

"Vũ? Isn't that a Vietnamese surname?" Leo asked.

Thiha Bo laughed a soft, sad laugh. "Yes. How do you say it? He's self-loathing."

Binh was watching their conversation silently, with wide, mournful eyes. He looked bereft, re-signed.

Anger surged in Leo's gut, and he suddenly wished Captain Vũ would show up. He balled his hands into fists. "I can help you. I *will* help you. Both of you. All of you," he promised in a fierce voice, shifting his gaze from the man at his side and the man in the cage.

~ ~ ~ ~ ~ ~ ~ ~ ~ ~ ~

Sasha glanced behind her as she and Mel walked at a quick clip to the car. They were still half a block away. And he was still back there. She touched Mel's elbow.

"The man who was watching us at the bistro— you're sure he was a white guy?"

Mel threw her a quizzical look. "Positive. Why?"

"Because there's a giant Asian man following us. Bald, ugly scar, wearing a suit that's about two sizes too small. He's been behind us since we left."

Mel swore under her breath and twisted her neck for a look at their new friend. "Well, he looks like bad news." Her tone was dry, but she picked up her pace.

Sasha had to agree with her assessment. She was pretty sure that the two of them could take him down if it came to that—between her Krav Maga training and Mel's Bureau training they should have enough tricks in their bag to beat up one thug in a street fight. But, call her crazy, she really didn't feel like getting into a brawl. For one thing, getting blood out of her pastel cotton dress would be a pain. For another, she wasn't exactly wearing running shoes.

She gave Mel a sidelong glance. The legat was wearing shoes that would have made Connelly proud—sensible low-heeled loafers. She reached down and removed one of her own stacked, high-heeled sandals, hopping on one foot as she did so. Then she removed the other.

Mel arched a brow at the sandals, which were now swinging from Sasha's right hand and then made a face at Sasha's bare feet. "These streets aren't exactly sanitary, you know."

"I'm up on my shots. I'm thinking that really big guys are usually pretty slow. Feel like running the rest of the way?"

Mel grinned at her and took off at full speed. Sasha followed, catching up to her about a hundred yards from the sedan.

"You're fast," she huffed out between breaths.

"Sprinter," Mel panted. "College track. Did we lose him?"

They kept jogging but turned to look back. He'd fallen well behind them and had dropped to his knees. Sasha hoped he was experiencing chest pains or a cramp or something equally unpleasant. But that hope was short-lived as he braced his right arm with his left and took aim.

"Swerve!" Mel yelled as she veered to the right. Sasha had already tucked and rolled across the filthy sidewalk, abandoning the sandals in the scrubby grass. The first shot whizzed between them and hit a metal street sign.

Sasha scrabbled to her feet and danced left then right, weaving an unpredictable pattern as she ran. Beside her Mel did the same. It was like being chased by an alligator.

Another bullet missed them. The car was just feet away. The man was a small, distant shape now. Sasha's heart slowed a half a beat. Unless he was a sharpshooter, which he clearly was not, he wasn't going to hit them at this distance. She kept zigzagging anyway. Better safe than sorry.

Mel dug into her purse and pulled out the car keys. She hit the remote key to unlock the doors and they threw themselves into the front seat. She jammed the key into the ignition with shaking hands and the engine roared to life. She peeled out, clipping a trashcan with the passenger side as she yanked on her seatbelt one-handed.

Sasha locked her own seatbelt and then exhaled. When her breathing returned to normal, she said, "Can I use your phone. I'll let Connelly know it's time to go."

Mel tossed her purse into Sasha's lap. As Sasha pawed through it for the cell phone, it began to ring. She dug it out.

"Look at that. He's calling us."

21.

T
O LEO'S SURPRISE, Sasha, and not Mel,
answered the legal attaché's mobile phone.

"Sasha? Is Mel there?" he asked.

His wife hesitated before answering. "She's a little ... busy ... at the moment. What's up?"

"I found the boat. I'm on it, actually—the boat
the woman was on when she was murdered. Her
name was Mina. And her killers were apparently
mercenaries hired by Thale." He waited, but Sasha
didn't react. Something was definitely wrong, but
whatever it was would have to wait until they took
care of the time-sensitive reason for his call. "Does
Mel have the power to authorize me to detain the

boat until she can get a law enforcement team out here?"

"Hang on."

He could hear their faint voices in murmured conversation as Sasha relayed his question and Mel answered it, and he wondered why Sasha hadn't simply handed the phone to Mel. It would have been quicker. A squealing noise that sounded suspiciously like tires laying down rubber filled his ear.

A moment later, Sasha was back on the line. "So, here's the thing. We have to leave town. Now. Something's come up. We'll come down to the dock and get you, but you've got to be ready to just jump in the car, okay? Once we're in the clear, Mel will reach out to Ron to mobilize the local police to deal with the boat."

"Are you joking? We have to secure the boat until someone can at least put the captain under arrest. And what do you mean 'in the clear'? Sasha, what's going on?"

She sighed. "Okay, so don't freak out. We're *fine*. But a man with a gun followed us out of the bistro and he's taken a few shots at us. *But* he's on foot and seems to be a terrible shot, *and* Mel is a great evasive driver. We're pretty sure we shook him, but we really need to get out of Dodge."

Leo promptly freaked out. "What? Someone tried to *kill* you? Who? Why? Are you sure you're okay?"

She spoke in the deliberate, calm and soothing voice that she used when one of the twins was having a meltdown. "We're fine, honestly. Mel caught some creep watching us at the restaurant. We both got a bad vibe about it and decided to leave. And apparently it's a good thing we did, since a giant, gun-wielding Thai man chased after us. But he was slow, and we outran him. The end. We're in the car on our way to get you. It's time to move on."

Leo bit his lip. An Asian giant trying to kill his wife was a legitimate problem, no doubt about it. But leaving the men on this boat and walking away was really not an option. They were effectively enslaved. He couldn't pretend he hadn't seen that.

Besides, Sasha was always getting irritated with him for acting as though she couldn't take care of herself. And she *was* with a federal agent, who seemed more than competent. He was silent as he tried to justify to himself what he was about to do.

"Connelly? Did you hear me? We're coming to get you. Be ready, okay?"

He glanced over at Binh, still crouched in the cage like an abused dog, and Thiha Bo, who was pointedly studying the ceiling, pretending not to listen to his end of the conversation. Slowly, he said, "I can't do that."

"What does that even mean?"

"It means you and Mel need to get out of town, stat, but I'm staying here. Get in touch with the embassy as soon as you can safely make the call. Have them send the police to the dock. Once the captain's been taken into custody and the crew members have been squared away, I'll get somebody to give me a lift to Bangkok. Ask Mel to text me the address where you end up staying, and I'll see you later tonight."

He could almost hear her thinking, trying to devise some other course of action, but they both knew there was no viable alternative.

"There's no point in my telling you this is a terrible idea, is there?"

"You already know the answer to that."

She gave a sad little laugh. "I do. So I guess I'll have to settle for telling you to please be careful."

"Hey, that's my line."

That at least earned him a genuine laugh before she said, "I'll see you tonight."

"I'll see you tonight," he echoed.

"And Connelly? I'm really glad you found the boat so Mina's murder won't go unpunished."

There were all sorts of atrocities happening on the ship that weren't going to go unpunished either—not if he had anything to say about it. But this wasn't the time to discuss it. "Me, too. I love you."

"I love you more," she whispered.

"Not possible." He ended the call and walked toward Thiha Bo with the phone still in his hands. He was going to need help once the captain returned. They had to devise some sort of action plan to maintain control of the boat until the cavalry arrived.

Before he could open his mouth to explain the situation, all hell broke loose.

Running feet pounded from every direction on the deck. Overlapping shouted commands and orders created a din that was even louder than the slap of running feet. Thiha Bo stared wide-eyed toward the sound of the chase.

"What's going on?" Leo asked.

The Burmese man shook his head. "You wait here. I'll find out." He eased the door open just a crack and slipped out into the hallway.

Leo pressed himself up against the wall behind the door in case Captain Vũ or another officer decided to check on the prisoner during the commotion and scanned the sparse room for something that could be pressed into duty as a weapon if need be. *Nothing*. He tensed when the door opened, ready to spring, but stopped himself when Thiha Bo hurried inside.

Thiha Bo headed straight across the room toward Binh and motioned for Leo to follow so he could fill them both in at the same time. He spoke first in English and then repeated the information in Vietnamese. "We're leaving. We were to stay here through the night and set a course in the morning, but Captain Vũ has returned in a rage. Something about two American women." He paused here and flicked his eyes toward Leo for a brief moment. "I couldn't make it all out. The order came down to work double time—we need to set sail as rapidly as we can."

Binh pinned his worried eyes on Leo, as if he was imploring him to do something to stop this.

Leo's pulse jumped. He couldn't let this ship leave the dock. But how was he supposed to stop an entire crew, alone and unarmed? He took a long, deep breath. "Do the men trust you? Could you organize them?" he asked Thiha Bo.

Thiha Bo titled his head. "Are you asking if I could convince them to mutiny?"

Leo hadn't really thought of it in terms of mutiny, but yes, that was what he was asking. "Yes."

Thiha Bo sighed. "They—we—are too frightened of the captain and the soldiers on the company's payroll. Plus, there's no time. Maybe, if I could talk to them, little by little, over time, they would grow brave. But not like this." He spread his hands wide in an apologetic gesture.

Leo gritted his teeth. The news was bad, but not surprising. "Okay, Plan B. Do you know where the boat's headed?"

Maybe he could get in touch with Mel, have her patch him through to Ron, and they could send out the Thai equivalent of the Coast Guard or the Navy to intercept the boat at sea. That was a long shot and much more complicated than his original plan. But he couldn't just do nothing and let them sail away.

Thiha Bo shook his head no. "No, but I know how we can find out. Come with me."

Thiha Bo bent beside Binh's cage and spoke to him through the bars in a low voice. Leo assumed he was telling the man they'd be back for him. Leo joined him at the edge of the cage and wrapped his fingers around the wires. He stared hard at Binh, then he turned to Thiha Bo. "Tell him to hold steady and stay calm."

A wide grin bloomed on Thiha Bo's worried face. "I don't need to tell him. His name means peaceful, even. So steady and calm is his nature."

With one more backward glance at Binh, Leo followed Thiha Bo out of the cabin and onto the deck.

As they raced across the open deck, the ship suddenly lurched, shuddering violently, and Thiha Bo pitched sideways into Leo, who had already lost his own footing.

Leo realized they were pulling away from the dock just as a crew member ran by him, his hands full of ropes, and knocked him into the railing with his shoulder. His wrists hit the top of the railing and he watched in horror as the satellite phone bounced out of his hands, flipped over the rail, and disappeared into the churning water below.

He didn't know how long he would have stood there, staring down at the murky sea, if Thiha Bo hadn't pulled him toward rickety stairs that led to the crew's sleeping chamber.

He was on a boat piloted by a murderer, racing out to sea with no gun, no phone, and no one who knew where he was.

He'd had better days.

22.

MEL REACHED UP and adjusted her rear-view mirror. Her hand trembled. "I don't see anyone behind us, do you?"

Sasha twisted in her seat and looked through the back window at the stretch of empty road behind them. "Nope. You lost him."

Mel let out a great *whoosh* of breath. "Oh, thank goodness. I've never been, you know, shot at before."

"You did great," Sasha assured her.

The legal attaché let her eyes slide away from the road and appraised Sasha for a moment. Sasha knew Mel was wondering how a civilian, a trial attorney, had stayed reasonably calm in the situation they'd just escaped and was now critiquing her performance.

"I *have* been shot at before," she explained.

Mel's eyes widened. "Okay, now I have about a million follow-up questions, but we need to pull off and call Ron."

She eased the car to the side of the road and parked behind a stand of scrubby trees, which would at least partially obscure the vehicle from view if anyone happened to drive by. Sasha scanned the highway from both directions while Mel checked in with her boss. She filled him in dispassionately, as though she were chased by gunmen on at least a weekly basis. Sasha admired her steely attitude.

After Mel began to explain about the boat docked back in Samut Prakan, her demeanor changed. It seemed that Ron was doing a lot of interrupting; and, from the agitated way Mel was drumming her fingernails on the steering wheel, Sasha suspected she didn't like what she was hearing.

"But, sir—" *Drum, drum, drum.*

"I think that—" *Drum, drum, drum.*

"No, sir—" *Drum, drum, drum.*

Mel stole a glance at Sasha then scrunched up her shoulders and made what sounded like the beginning of an impassioned plea. "Please, Ron—"

She deflated like a forlorn balloon. "I understand. Yes, sir. Will do."

She jabbed the button to end the call and turned to Sasha. "You're not going to like this."

That sounded about right. So far, there was precious little that Sasha liked about the 'exciting shore side excursion in exotic Thailand,' promised in her cruising itinerary.

"Just tell me. Don't bother sugarcoating it to make Ron sound good."

Mel twisted her mouth into a wry smile. "Actually, he's probably right—as irritating as that is. He wants me to take you back to your cruise ship."

"What? No."

Mel raised both hands. "Hang on. Hear me out. Despite how it must look to you, Thailand isn't the Wild West. It does have a drug-trafficking problem, the usual purse snatchings and thefts that always pop up in tourist destinations, and the drugging of drinks that I told you about. But it's actually highly unusual to be chased through the streets by a shooter. Whatever you saw out in the gulf, it must be tied to something bigger than an isolated murder. We don't know what that is. And that means

Ron and I can't protect you. It's not like we're in a Bureau field office with backup. We're attached to the embassy. It's a diplomatic outpost. And whatever this woman's death has stirred up, it's going to have political ramifications that we'll have to manage."

Mel paused for a breath. Sasha interjected, "Ron didn't say the murder of this Mina person stirred up anything. Connelly and I stirred it up, right?"

Mel shrugged and didn't answer, which Sasha took as a yes.

"That doesn't really matter. We can't guarantee your safety. Ron pointed out that we're on the only really viable route to Bangkok. It would be exceedingly easy—child's play—for a reasonably connected criminal enterprise to send someone from a village up ahead to ambush us. Look around. There's nowhere to go."

Sasha frowned. It was true. The highway, such as it was, was a single ribbon running along the coast. There didn't appear to be many exits or alternate roads.

"So, how's it safer to turn around and drive back toward Samut Prakan? We'd have to go right past the turn off. What if there's someone waiting there to ambush us?"

Mel nodded. "Right." She paused and cleared her throat. "So, um, Ron's calling Sacred Lotus. He's going to arrange for someone from *The Water Lily* to come out here and escort you back to the ship."

Sasha choked out a laugh. "Wait, so to ensure my personal safety, the highest representative of Federal Bureau of Investigations in this entire country wants to hand me off to a gopher from a cruise ship? Is this a joke?"

Mel wasn't laughing.

Suddenly Sasha's lawyer-brain woke up and everything clicked into place. "Of course. This is to avoid liability. If I happen to get ambushed and killed while some crew member's ferrying me back to *The Water Lily*, Ron's hands are clean. The Bureau won't be responsible for my safety at that point."

Mel was silent.

"Mel, this is stupid."

"It's out of my hands. I'm really sorry. I'm authorized to stay here with you until someone employed by Sacred Lotus Cruises shows up. Then I'm supposed to head back to Samut Prakan and find your husband."

Connelly.

"How does the Bureau's desperate need to deny involvement impact him? Is Ron at least going to send the police to the dock?"

"I understand your frustration, I do. But you have to believe me, Ron's a pro. He's going to make sure that captain's taken into custody as quickly as possible. And then he'll have someone bring Leo back to the ship. It's a different situation with your husband because he's an agent himself ... or a former agent? A contractor? Whatever he is. He's not a civilian."

Sasha gritted her teeth and bit down hard to prevent herself from saying something unkind and regrettable. After she had her temper firmly in hand, she let out a breath.

"He's alone, with no backup. He doesn't speak the language. And he's investigating a murder. Regardless of his current or former relationship to your employer, any halfway decent attorney will have a slam dunk case if he so much as gets a scratch. And I'm a damned sight better than halfway decent at my job, just so you know." Her voice shook with a potent mixture of frustration, anger, and fear.

Mel blinked. "I understand." She placed a hesitant hand on Sasha's arm. "He'll be fine. From everything I've heard, he's also damned good at his job." Then a thought struck her. "He *is* armed, right?"

Sasha shook her head miserably. "No. He's not carrying a gun. All he has is that fancy phone of his."

They sat in silence for a moment as Mel processed that piece of news. Then she said with forced cheerfulness. "We should call him and bring him up to speed."

She punched his number into her phone without waiting for Sasha to respond.

"Here, I'll put it on speaker," she offered.

The tinny sound of ringing filled the car. Connelly's phone rang and rang. And rang. And rang.

With each trill, Sasha's heart sank closer and closer to her stomach.

23.

THE MAN RETURNED to the room in a foul mood and with a thunderous face. He ignored Jan, who had roused himself long enough to watch the Thai storm into the room, and picked up the telephone handset.

Jan reclined on the couch and tried to tune out the man's angry telephone call. He didn't understand the language well enough to follow the substance of the call, but the man's tone was sufficiently agitated that it interrupted Jan's pleasant, meandering thoughts and distracted him from his high.

As Jan half-listened, he realized the man was talking to one of his bosses. Despite the visible rage in his posture and body language, his voice was controlled and somehow deferential. The fact that the bodyguard/drug dealer/enforcer was speaking to someone at Thale unleashed a worry that nibbled at the edges of Jan's drug euphoria, bit by bit, until it had been devoured entirely.

Great. Now he was in a foul mood, too.

He slumped back and crossed his arms, staring at the Thai until he finished his conversation. When the man returned the phone to the desk, he immediately met Jan's gaze. "It's time for you to go."

"Go?" Jan gave him a look of confusion. "I'm paid up through the night—until morning. That's the arrangement."

"Well, the arrangement's changed. The new arrangement is that you need to get out. Now." He slammed his palm down flat on the desk for emphasis.

The sharp noise startled Jan, and he jumped. He considered requesting a refund. But, after taking a closer look at the man's murderous expression, he decided that, given the circumstances, it would be prudent not to stand on principle. "Of course. Could you arrange transportation for me back to Laem Chabang?"

He would have to return to the ship. He didn't dare risk partying anywhere public. The entire point of reserving the room at Bar Pavot was the privacy it afforded him.

As the man considered Jan's request, a satisfied expression replaced his scowl. "I will. Yes, that will work."

Jan blinked in surprise at the way the man had acquiesced so easily. Something about his words made Jan think the agreement would come with strings attached. He waited.

"You say the woman who is making the trouble is a passenger on your ship, yeah?"

The woman. This was all about that blasted Connelly woman.

"One of them is," he answered carefully. "The small, dark-haired woman is a passenger, yes. I believe the other woman is attached to the American embassy. You didn't catch up with them, did you?" The man's frenetic anger suddenly made sense.

The Thai gritted his teeth. He didn't answer the question. "The boss is going to need your help in taking care of her. Your driver will fill you in."

Jan's anxiety exploded into full-blown panic. "What do you mean by taking care of her? I can't be involved in this. You need to tell them—"

"I don't need to tell them anything. You're already involved. Now gather your things and go. Panit will be waiting at the back exit to take you to the port. I have instructions to shut down operations until this blows over. They're not happy about the effect this is going to have on the bottom line, captain. So, if I were you, I'd do everything in my power to help clean up this mess quickly." With that, he turned his back on Jan and walked to the wall safe to return the gun and money he'd removed earlier.

Jan hesitated with the rosewood box still in his hand. He still had four cigarettes left and many hours until he would need to pilot *The Water Lily*. But he also had rules. And one of those rules was that he didn't indulge outside Bar Pavot when he was in Thailand. He had a similar rule for similar establishments in other ports. And, if Thale really did plan to drag him into this unsavory business, he'd need to keep his wits about him. But, then, he'd also need a way to calm his nerves, and nothing relaxed him more completely than this. He weighed the box in his hand, debating internally.

After brief moment that seemed to him to stretch interminably, he made his decision and cleared his throat. "Friend, will you be so kind as to secure these for me until I can return?"

Surprise registered in the man's dark eyes, as though he'd judged Jan to be no different from some out-of-control addict living on the street, but he didn't remark on it. He simply gave a short, quick nod and reached out his hand to take the box. Jan handed over his drugs and watched as the man locked them away in the safe. Then he headed out through the back exit that led to a parking lot in the alley, forcing himself to push away thoughts of what Thale would require of him. He tried to appear as if he were unconcerned with what lie ahead. He hoped the man didn't notice his legs shaking as he walked away.

~ ~ ~ ~ ~ ~ ~ ~ ~ ~

Sasha and Mel sat in silence. Sasha didn't know what was going through the other woman's mind, but her own brain was a maelstrom of worry. They tried over and over to reach Connelly, but he wasn't answering his phone. A sour, sick taste filled her throat. She distracted herself from her rising nausea by scanning the road. After several minutes, she spotted the white SUV approaching from the south. She touched Mel's arm. "Look. Someone's coming."

They both leaned forward, straining as the vehicle drew closer to determine whether it contained a friend or an enemy.

Sasha squinted, made out a tasteful lotus design painted on the side of the vehicle, and relaxed. "It's someone from the cruise ship."

"Are you sure?" Mel's hand floated toward the locked glove compartment, where Sasha was fairly certain her Bureau-issued firearm was stowed away.

She nodded. "I recognize the logo."

"Still, let me go first. Just in case." Mel leaned over and unlocked the glove box, and Sasha pretended not to notice the key shaking in her hand. She removed a handgun and checked the safety. Then she squared her shoulders and stepped out of the car.

The SUV came to a stop just at the edge of the shoulder of the road. The driver cut the engine and walked around to the front of his vehicle. Sasha relaxed her shoulders. It was Bruce.

She grabbed her purse, pushed open the passenger side, and stepped out onto the dusty shoulder. The sound of her door closing caught Mel's attention and earned Sasha a sidelong look of displeasure.

"It's okay, I know him. He's my assigned butler."

Mel exhaled loudly, her breath shaky, and holstered her gun. "Butler, huh? Must be a pretty nice boat."

Sasha raised her hand in greeting. "Hi, Bruce," she called.

Bruce waved back. A look of concern was painted across his face.

The three met at a point roughly halfway between the cars. Mel turned to Sasha. "I don't want to stand out here in the open and have a long goodbye. I promise I'll track down your husband and get him back to you in one piece. And, like I said, Ron and I *will* take care of ... that other matter."

"Thanks, Mel. Despite the circumstances, it's been nice meeting you." Sasha meant it.

She extended her hand to shake goodbye, but to her surprise the legal attaché grabbed her and swept her into a fierce, quick hug. Mel released her as quickly as she'd embraced her.

Mel turned to Bruce. "Take good care of her."

Bruce, expertly hiding any confusion he might have at Mel or Sasha's behavior, bowed his head slightly. "I certainly shall, madam. It is, after all, my job."

And just like that, the Embassy's handoff of an American citizen was complete. Mel returned to her sedan. Sasha and Bruce walked in silence to the SUV. When they reached the passenger side, he opened the door for her with a little flourish.

She waited to speak until he'd buckled his seatbelt, started the engine, and had executed the U-turn that would take them back toward the port at Laem Chabang and the waiting ship. "Did they tell you why I need to go back to the ship?"

Mel had insisted that Ron wouldn't provide any details to Sacred Lotus or the crew of *The Water Lily*, but Sasha knew he would've told someone *something*. She was curious what Bruce had been told.

He shifted his gaze from the road for a moment and studied her face. "I was contacted at the monastery and asked to pick you up because you're having a medical issue. I understand you would feel more comfortable being treated by the ship's doctor than by a local physician. A wise decision; Dr. Harmon is top-notch."

Sasha *hmmed* quietly. As far as cover stories went, she had to give Ron credit. Needing medical attention was a plausible feint and had the added benefit that most people would hesitate to pry for details.

After a moment of silence, Bruce said, "Will we be picking up Mr. Connelly somewhere along the way?"

The worry and fear that Sasha had been working so hard to hide rushed to the surface and she felt the blood drain from her face. She had to swallow hard before she answered because her throat had gone bone dry. She let out a long breath then said, "He'll be meeting us back on the ship." Then she squeezed her eyes shut and sent up a silent prayer that her statement would prove true.

"I see." Bruce returned his attention to the road.

After several silent moments, Sasha's eyes popped open. "I just realized you had to cut short your retreat. I'm so sorry, Bruce."

"Please, Mrs. McCandless-Connelly. It's of no consequence."

"Of course is it," she insisted. "This is your leave time. You were looking forward to meditating with the monks."

"I was," he agreed. "But a person must find peace everywhere. Otherwise, he will not find peace anywhere."

She considered his words for a moment, wondering if they were some sort of Zen koan or his own personal philosophy. Either way, he seemed to be unperturbed by having to cut short his retreat to fetch her. The more she thought about his pro-nouncement, the more she began to wonder if the statement was intended as a message for her. She eyed him closely, but his face was an inscrutable mask. Finally, she leaned back against the headrest and focused on the sound of her own breathing—in and out, in and out—in an effort to calm her nerves and still her mind. She'd find her peace if it killed her.

24.

CAPTAIN JAN VAN METIER shut the door of the black Lexus firmly and walked smartly up the ramp to his ship without a backward glance. In the altogether likely event that any of the crew or passengers who'd stayed behind saw him approach the ship, it was critically important to act as though he'd been dropped off by a hired chauffeur and not a street thug who had just attempted to intimidate and threaten him into doing his employer's bidding.

He squared his jaw and his shoulders. He'd deal with Thale from the privacy of his quarters. For now, his priority was to make a strong show of authority.

Julia Otterbein trotted over to him as he board-ed *The Water Lily*. "Captain van Metier, sir, is every-thing okay?" she asked, slightly breathless.

He arched a silver eyebrow in response to the somewhat personal question coming from his sen-ior hostess.

"Oh, I'm sorry. I do apologize," she said, flus-tered. She proceeded to babble in an apparent ef-fort to unruffle his feathers. "Did the American Embassy call you? I assured the gentleman who contacted us that we would take care of Ms. McCandless-Connelly. He didn't need to disturb you, as well." Her perfectly lipsticked mouth turned down in an irritated frown.

Jan felt as though he had a golf ball stuck in his windpipe. "Mrs. Connelly?" he wheezed. "What in the blue blazes does Mrs. Connelly have to do with anything?"

Julia's eyes narrowed at his deliberate use of the personal title that he knew full-well the woman didn't use. He pretended not to notice. He could not have cared less if some female lawyer preferred a hyphenated mouthful. He'd call her by her hus-band's surname if he liked.

Julia smoothed out her expression and gave him a tentative smile. "I must be confused. I thought you might have received a call, too. Ms.

McCandless-Connelly took ill on the road to Bangkok and sought assistance from the United States Embassy. They asked that we come fetch her and bring her back here for medical attention."

"Is that so? She's on board now?" Wheels had begun to turn in Jan's mind. Perhaps he could broker a compromise with Thale.

"Yes, sir. Bruce Totten was kind enough to cut short his shore leave and go get her. Dr. Harmon looked her over. My understanding is he offered her something for her nerves. She's gone to her cabin to rest."

This could work. This could actually work.

In his excitement, he nearly cheered, but he caught himself just in time. "Very good. Is there anything else she requires?" he asked in a stiffly formal voice.

Julia shook her head. "Bruce is taking care of her. She did ask to borrow one of the ship's mobile telephones. She and her husband became separated somehow, and she's anxious to reach him."

Mr. Connelly, the broad-shouldered, hulking husband, wasn't onboard? This opportunity was getting better and better.

"Call off the hunt for a loaner phone. Tell Bruce I'll personally see to it that Mrs. Connelly gets what she needs."

Julia's eyebrows shot up in surprise at his offer to involve himself in such a mundane passenger request, but he turned on his heel and hurried away before she could comment. He needed to contact Thale as soon as possible. He forced himself to walk at a brisk pace despite the fact that he desperately wanted to break into a run.

When he reached the door to his suite, he had the key card ready in his hand. He passed it in front of the reader and slipped inside his private quarters before another crew member had the chance to waylay him. He removed his jacket and hung it in the closet, smoothing out the few wrinkles that had developed. Then he located the slip of paper that Panit had given to him in the car.

The driver had scrawled a telephone number in slanted handwriting; no name. He punched the digits into his telephone. While he listened to the ringing, he leaned against his bureau and steadied his breathing. He had one chance to convince Thale to follow his plan. One chance to protect his career, his reputation, and his passengers. He exhaled.

"Yes?" A voice growled.

To his surprise, the speaker answered in English. To his further surprise, he recognized the voice. It was the man who ran the backroom at Bar

Pavot. He'd expected to reach someone at Thale's headquarters.

"Van Metier?" the man pressed, his impatience plain.

"Oh, yes, sorry. I just realized I don't know your name."

"No, you don't." The man paused for a beat. "You can call me *Thān*."

Thān. Thai for 'sir,' even he knew that much. He pushed aside the niggle of irritation at the man's arrogance. He needed an ally, so '*Thān*' would have to do.

"Very good, Thān."

"You're calling because you've reconsidered? Good."

He hesitated. "Not exactly. I have a counter-proposal." Surely, even this criminal understood that he couldn't possibly agree to Thale's demand: no captain worth his salt would acquiesce to go along with the hijacking of his ship by armed men on the open sea. His passengers would panic; someone could be injured—or worse. The damage to Sacred Lotus's reputation from such a scandal would be severe. And his career would almost certainly not survive the inquiry that would follow.

"This isn't a negotiation," Thān barked.

"Please, hear me out."

The only response was a grunt. Jan decided to treat that as a 'yes' and began his pitch. "As I understand the issue, Thale—"

"No names!"

"Right, apologies. Your employer needs to, err, neutralize a single passenger. The American woman."

"Yes. And our plan will accomplish that."

"I have a simpler plan. Right now, the ship is mostly empty. All but a handful of the passengers and many of the crew are off on excursions to Bangkok until mid-morning tomorrow."

"We're aware." His tone suggested the captain had better get to the point more quickly.

Jan continued hurriedly, "Right, right. But the woman you need is onboard now. Her embassy contacted us, claiming she'd taken ill and required medical treatment. When I returned, she was already here. She's in her cabin, apparently, resting. Her husband is still on land, presumably there in Samut Prakan. But the ship is nearly deserted. Send your men now."

"Hijackings occur at sea."

Jan shook his head at the lack of creative thinking. "Come, man, then make it a kidnapping. If they board quietly, I may not even be alerted. And I assure you, I'll take my time contacting port security once I am made aware of the issue. It'll make the entire operation far easier for your men if we're stationary."

After a long silence, the man said, "Make sure she's easy to find."

"I'll personally see to it that her door is unlocked."

Thān grunted again and hung up without another word.

Jan closed his eyes and exhaled slowly. The difficult part was over.

~ ~ ~ ~ ~ ~ ~ ~ ~ ~

Sasha paced around the stateroom like an agitated lioness. She'd been back on *The Water Lily* for over an hour and so far Bruce had stopped by three separate times, bearing herbal tea, the pills Dr. Harmon had prescribed for her 'nerves' (which she'd promptly pitched in the wastepaper basket under the bathroom vanity), and an aromatherapy pillow Julia had liberated from the spa's gift shop. What she really needed, she'd reminded him as gently as she'd been able to manage, was a cellular phone capable of making calls to the mainland. She hadn't bothered to ensure she'd have coverage on her phone; she'd figured she could just use Connelly's phone when she needed to make calls. Now, they were separated, and her phone was no more useful than a paperweight.

She paused in her stalking long enough to shake out her hands and take several deep breaths. If Bruce couldn't get a phone for her, she'd simply have to engage in some self-help. Surely someone had left an unsecured phone somewhere on the ship. She'd 'borrow' it and return it before anyone was the wiser.

The prospect of *doing* something—anything—immediately reduced her anxiety level. She laced up her running shoes, pulled her hair into a low ponytail, and grabbed her keycard off the antique desk near the door. She was halfway out the door when she nearly bounced off a uniformed chest. She looked up and met Captain van Metier's steely gaze.

Great.

"Mrs. Connelly, are you quite sure you should be out of bed?"

"Pardon?" Sasha asked, certain she'd misheard him.

"Julia tells me that Dr. Harmon recommended that you rest."

"Oh, right. I just wanted to get some fresh air." She tilted her head toward the door in the universal signal for 'get out of my way.'

He frowned down at her and continued to block her path. "I don't think that's advisable."

She gave him a blank look. "I'm fine. Really. If you'll excuse me ..." she trailed off and gestured for him to move aside because he really was blocking her path.

He pressed a rugged-looking mobile phone into her hands. "I understand you need to make some calls."

She was instantly glad she'd resisted the urge to shoulder him out of the way. "Thanks so much," she chirped, as she grabbed the phone and whirled back into her room.

~ ~ ~ ~ ~ ~ ~ ~ ~ ~ ~

Jan rubbed his chin in thought. Given the American woman's penchant for wandering around the ship, overriding her door locks so that the door was unlocked might cause more problems than it solved. But how else to ensure Thale's men could get to her? He grimaced at the thought of what would happen if the men who stormed the ship didn't find her in her room.

He sighed. Much as he might have liked to, he couldn't very well lock her *in*. The electronic system didn't work that way. It was out of his hands. The telephone he'd given her did have an active GPS locator, but he wasn't entirely sure how granular that data would be. He'd have to hope for the best.

He passed his key fob over her doorknob, deactivating the lock, then slipped the fob into his pocket and strolled away. Once he reached the sun deck, he took out his own cell phone and called Thān. "Your men should hurry. Her door's unlocked, but I can't guarantee she'll stay inside. I'll try to keep tabs on her. That's the best I can do."

"Don't worry. They're professionals."

Jan hesitated. "They need to remove her from the ship before they ... do whatever it is they plan to do."

"The phrase you're searching for is 'kill her.' We need to silence her. And, yes, they've been told not to make a mess on your precious cruise ship."

This time, Jan ended the call before the Thai could hang up on him.

25.

DEREK DIDN'T LIKE surprises. He'd been prepared to hijack the cruise ship on its way to Ho Chi Minh City and shoot the woman during the chaos. That had been the plan. The sudden change of strategy irked him and pricked at him like a splinter as he steered the gleaming black personal watercraft vehicle through the roiling waves.

He also didn't particularly like driving the PWC—especially not when the sea was this choppy. He tightened his grip on the handlebars. He risked a quick glance at Austin. Austin, who kept a picture of his motorcycle pinned up over his bunk like he was some lovesick GI and the bike was his girl back home, was grinning like an idiot. Of course he was.

"Yee-haw!" Austin shouted.

Derek could barely hear him over the deafening thunder of their racing engines. He shook his head, sending a spray of water droplets into his own face. His partner might view the unusual transportation as a perk of this particular job, but he didn't. The job itself was straightforward enough: grab the girl, take her out to sea, kill her, and dump the body. It was just all this action hero bullcrap that was rubbing him the wrong way. But Thale had offered them a juicy premium for piloting PWCs, squeezing themselves into ridiculous wetsuits, and boarding a docked boat to silence a witness.

Of course, the whole reason they even *had* to silence her was Thale's own sloppiness. He should have just listened to his gut in the first place and insisted they shoot the Malaysian chick away from the cruise ship. *Shoulda, coulda, woulda. It was too late now.*

Derek spotted *The Water Lily* docked right where they'd been told they'd find it. He cut his engine and slashed his finger across his neck, signaling for Austin to do the same.

They bobbed closer to the hull of the cruise ship. Austin tossed his sandbag anchor into the water, and Derek followed his lead.

They'd been told to board the ship by climbing its side, being sure to stay out of sight of the port workers, which was easy enough to say. He eyed the massive ship. "How the devil are we supposed to get the girl off without being seen?" he grumbled, more to himself than to Austin.

Austin answered him anyway. "They said take her off the boat alive. Nobody said anything about her being conscious."

Derek had to hand it to him—every once in a while a pearl of wisdom half-buried in a clump of Skoal fell out of Austin's mouth. He removed his suction cup contraption from his backpack and eyed it skeptically. "Here goes nothing."

He'd been hoping for grappling hooks but he'd been unable to find any lying around the armory. Austin swore the suction cups would work to scale the side of the ship and would have the added bonus of being nearly silent. Derek hoisted himself and started spidering his way up. Austin stuck himself to the boat a few feet away and also scuttled up the slick steel hull toward the lower deck.

Derek settled into a rhythm. *Stick, stick, climb, climb. Stick, stick, climb, climb.* He scaled the side as quickly as he could. Nothing made a guy feel more vulnerable than being splayed out against the side of a ship. He reached a sort of lip or shelf that was cut out for the lifeboats and used it to gain a toe-hold to pull himself up and over the railing.

Then he dropped down on to the deck to survey the immediate vicinity. Austin landed beside him in a crouch. As promised, the cruise ship was near-ly deserted, although Derek imagined passengers would have little reason to be on this deck, which housed the mechanicals and a dizzying maze of color-coded piping. They sneaked along the bul-wark to a set of stairs. The centerpiece of *The Water Lily* was a sleek, glass elevator, but using it would be the equivalent of announcing their presence through a megaphone. So, they hoofed it.

The woman's suite was on the ninth deck, ac-cording to their contact at Thale. Derek kept one hand on his firearm and gripped the railing with the other as he mounted the stairs. He paused at the landing to the fifth deck to catch his breath. Austin stopped behind him and let out a low whis-tle.

He turned, irritated, to tell Austin to shut up and felt his jaw drop open when he saw what had caught Austin's attention. "Is that a casino?"

"Yup. Looks like there's some fancy theater, too. Panit said up on the top deck where the pools are there's a tennis court and golfing center, too."

This was a far cry from the roach-infested armory barracks. The entire ship screamed—well, whispered politely—of excess and wealth. These people had money, real money. Wheels began to turn in Derek's mind about a future freelance gig. He kept his mouth firmly shut. Austin wasn't his first choice for a partner on something self-directed and potentially wildly lucrative.

He stared down at the opulent casino entrance for another moment then shook himself to attention. "Come on. We need to get the woman and get out of here." He resumed the climb up the stairs, reluctantly, with Austin huffing along behind him. He made a note to add some cardiovascular training to his workouts. He lifted weights with a few of the guys back on the armory boat to kill the time, but he needed to do some running or something— he could feel his lungs burning as he continued up the stairs.

Finally, they reached the ninth deck and he leaned forward, hands braced on his knees, and waited for his heart rate to slow. Beside him, Austin rested against a half-wall, panting.

"What's the suite number again?" Derek asked once his breathing was back to normal.

"Uh, 46." Austin was reading off a scrap of paper. "On the port side. Is that left?"

"Yes."

They snaked around to the left side of the ship. They still hadn't seen a soul. Derek was beginning to think this might turn out to be an easy enough job, after all. Even if they did have to haul an adult woman down the side of the ship with them.

He paused outside a door marked with a discreet bronze '46' and nodded to Austin. Austin reached for his gun and nodded back.

Derek tested the doorknob and it yielded. He yanked it wide open and burst inside. Austin was right behind him, his piece drawn.

~ ~ ~ ~ ~ ~ ~ ~ ~ ~

Leo squatted and rocked back on his heels the way he'd seen the other men do. He kept his head bowed over the mesh net he was mending—or more accurately, pretending to mend—and made eye contact with no one. The T-shirt and shorts that Thiha Bo had somehow procured for him fit poorly because he was so much larger than any of the other men on the boat. Attempting to blend in with the others would only work for so long. He wouldn't pass anything more than a cursory glance. So he stayed alert, ready for someone to raise the alarm that an intruder was on board.

But, as the hours crawled by, he realized none of the men crammed into the cabin with him were going to report him to the captain. To a man, they kept their shoulders hunched and their eyes on their work. There was no chatter, no laughter. Nothing but fear. When two scrawny men walked into the room with a large metal pot, everyone put down their netting and picked up the nearest bowl. So he did the same. The bowl was dirty and cracked, flecked with bits of dried rice. The men with the pot made the rounds, filling each bowl with a scoop of rice and a ladle of watery fish stew. Leo eyed the fish with concern. All around him, the men used their fingers to scoop the hot food into their mouths, rapidly, as if they were ravenous.

He waited until the men had moved on, then he nudged his bowl toward the rail-thin man seated next to him. The man's eyes lit up and he grabbed it two-handed as if he feared Leo would reconsider. He smiled and bobbed his head. Leo noticed a fresh cut that ran behind the man's ear down to his neck. Sticky blood and dirt clung to the opening.

He touched that spot behind his own ear and gestured toward the man's cut. He paused in his eating and pantomimed swinging something with great force—a stick, a whip? Who knew? But it was clear he'd been beaten for some real or imagined infraction. Leo nodded and lowered his gaze back to the floor.

Sweat stung his eyes. The acrid odor of men who'd been at sea for months on end mixed with the stench of old fish assaulted his nostrils. He blinked away the sweat and tried to breathe through the smell. The horror of the life these men were trapped in clawed at him. He picked up his needle and net and returned to the task at hand.

A sharp whistle followed by a hiss near his right ear startled him. The thick darning needle slipped in his hands and he stabbed himself. He swore under his breath and shook his fingers while he looked around for the source of the noise.

Thiha Bo was crouched in the shadows behind the bucket that served as the makeshift bathroom for twenty-odd men. Leo let his net fall to the floor and crept toward the Burmese man.

"Did you find out where we're headed?" Leo asked in a low voice.

Thiha Bo nodded and whispered back, "I heard some talk." He gestured for Leo to follow him down a dark, narrow hallway.

Leo scanned the cabin but no one seemed to be paying any particular attention to them or their conversation. He ducked his head to avoid a beam and slipped into the corridor. He followed a few steps behind Thiha Bo, who pushed open a splintered door and led him into what appeared to be a supply closet. Nets, buckets, and hooks were haphazardly strewn on the floor and shelves. Leo squeezed in beside the smaller man and pulled the door shut so that it was open only a crack, just enough to let in a sliver of dim light.

"The captain was speaking to somebody on his radio." Thiha Bo took a breath. "He was saying we'd be in gray waters in less than an hour if we maintained our speed."

"Gray waters? What does that mean?"

Leo waited as the man pursed his lips and searched for the English words to explain the concept. He spoke slowly, gesturing with his hands. "There are parts of the Gulf of Siam—you would call it the Gulf of Thailand—where the boundaries are disputed. Thailand and Cambodia, these two have the most disagreements. But also, Malaysia and Vietnam. There are competing claims. There are also treaties or agreements among the countries, but there are many tensions. So there is a gray area where it is not clear who is the owner."

Leo considered the possible ramifications of a maritime territorial dispute. "So, if the police in Thailand received a report of a crime on this ship, would the authorities pursue Captain Vũ into these gray waters?"

Thiha Bo wrinkled his brow. "I do not think so, no. The navy would not want to risk ... I am not sure how to say it."

"An international incident?"

"Yes, an international incident."

Leo's stomach clenched. So much for Mel sending in the troops. He thought for a moment. "But we aren't in gray waters, yet."

"No, we are not," Thiha Bo agreed in a puzzled voice.

"I need to stop Captain Vũ from entering the contested area."

"Stop him? No, that's not possible."

Leo could barely see Thiha Bo in the shadowy closet, but he could feel the man's worry radiating from him in palpable waves. He was scared.

This wasn't the time to push him. Instead he said, "Can you take me to Binh?"

He hesitated. "It will be dangerous now. So many people are on the boat."

"Please, Thiha Bo." Leo stared at him unblinkingly until, even in the near-darkness, the other man was forced to look away. Leo knew he could find the room where Binh was being held on his own—no problem. But he needed a translator. And a chance to convince Thiha Bo to help him organize a mutiny.

The Burmese man sighed. "Yes, of course."

Leo pushed open the door and gestured for Thiha Bo to lead the way.

26.

ASHA WATCHED FROM a teak lounge chair on Elli and Oliver Kurck's veranda on Deck Eleven as two armed men wearing black wetsuits stalked down the corridor and forced their way into her suite, situated catty-corner and two levels down on Deck Nine. Beside her, Elli gasped.

"Shhh," Sasha said without taking her eyes off the scene below.

It would be virtually impossible for the men to hear Elli, as the Kurcks' suite was two decks up from Sasha and Connelly's and around a corner. But, all the same, it was a risk she'd rather not take.

"Elli, you should go back inside," she suggested.

"Are you coming?" Elli whispered.

"No. I want to watch and see what they do next." She spoke in an even voice that belied the frenetic drumbeat of her heart.

"Then I'm staying with you."

Sasha shifted her gaze away from her stateroom door long enough to glance at the Finnish woman beside her. Elli's face was the palest white imaginable and her blue eyes were wide with fear. The contrast was particularly stark against her shoulders, which were bare, blotchy, and beet red under her loose cotton tank top.

Elli had stayed back from the Sacred Lotus-sponsored excursion to Bangkok because she'd had an allergic reaction to the almond massage oil used during her spa treatment.

When Dr. Harmon had checked in on her after her first antihistamine treatment, he'd mentioned that Sasha was also onboard, so Elli had popped down to invite her up to her balcony for some cucumber water and company.

Still unable to reach Connelly and well on her way to working herself into a panic, Sasha had jumped at the chance. Now she desperately wished she'd thought to bring along the cell phone that Captain van Metier had lent her. But she'd left it lying on the highly polished cherry table near the glass doors, where it was doing her absolutely no good.

"Does your phone work here?"

"I'm not sure," Elli said. "I tried to call Oliver earlier to ask how the Golden Buddha tour at Wat Traimit had gone but I couldn't get through." She gnawed at her lower lip. "Why are there men with guns in your room?"

Good question, Sasha thought. Although she knew *why*—or at least she thought she did—it was the *how* that troubled her. The most likely explanation was that there was a leak at the Embassy; and that was bad news. If Ron and Mel couldn't be trusted, she and Connelly were in hot water— boiling hot water.

Elli was watching her face, waiting for an answer.

"I saw something I shouldn't have. A crime. I think those men are here to silence me."

Elli's face grew even paler and her eyes grew even wider. Sasha could see the blue-green veins throbbing near her temple as she swallowed hard and said, "We need to find Captain van Metier."

Sasha worked to maintain a neutral expression. She was unimpressed by the captain's responsiveness, to put it mildly. He'd probably tell her that she *must* be mistaken—the gunmen couldn't *possi-*

bly have entered her room without a keycard—and leave it at that.

The gunmen, who most assuredly had entered her room, chose that moment to exit it. The taller, stockier of the two was having a fit of rage. He pulled back and kicked the railing with a great deal of force, and then starting yelping in pain and hopping on one foot. The thinner man leaned against the wall and watched his partner. Even from this distance, Sasha could see his mouth curving in amusement.

So one kept his emotions in check. The other was volatile.

She realized she was filing this information away because she expected to need it. And that fact made a shiver run up her spine. "I don't suppose you happen to have any weapons?" she asked in a casual voice.

Elli blinked. "No." Her voice shook.

"I really need you to go inside," Sasha said softly.

Elli stiffened her spine and straightened her shoulders. "Absolutely not."

Sasha exhaled and might have argued with her, but instead she pointed to the glass column that housed the elevator. The car was moving. It stopped on the ninth floor, and the mirrored doors parted. The men raced toward it.

Captain van Metier stepped out to confront the gunmen. She waited for a bevy of officers to rush out after him, but no one followed. She shook her head. What was he thinking coming alone? She leaned over the balcony and peered down into the center core of the ship. Now, they would be close enough that the sound of her voice and Elli's would carry down to them. She raised a finger to her lips to warn Elli to be silent.

Captain van Metier addressed the men in a low voice. The calmer one, who Sasha decided must be in charge, gestured back toward her room and then pointed at the captain's chest. Captain van Metier raised his hands skyward in a gesture of bewilderment. The less controlled of the two intruders waved his gun around for emphasis while he shouted. The wind carried a snippet of his yelling up to the balcony, but the words made no sense: "Thale can find another dragon shuttle if it needs to."

Dragon shuttle? She turned the phrase over, trying to tease out a meaning, but failed. And could 'Thale' be the same Thale that owned the fishing boat? Mel had said the family was everywhere.

After a moment, the captain nodded curtly. Sasha caught just a glimpse of his somber expression before he walked out of sight, trailed by the two men.

"Why didn't he detain them? Surely there's a brig," Elli said in a hushed voice.

"I'm sure there is. But he doesn't appear to be armed. And I'm guessing standard operating procedure is probably to try to negotiate with pirates." That wouldn't have been *her* first reaction, but Sacred Lotus probably had a team of lawyers, public relations consultants, and insurance brokers who'd laid out step-by-step the least expensive, most effective way to end a hijacking. Probably on a PowerPoint presentation.

"Do you really think they're pirates? What on Earth—" Elli began.

Her question was cut off by the crackle of a loudspeaker system coming to life. Captain van Metier's voice boomed and echoed across the mostly empty ship; his tone was grave and firm, but measured. "Attention, passengers. This is your captain speaking. This is not an exercise. We have an urgent situation. Please follow my instructions to the letter. All men, both crew members and guests, please report to the tiki bar on the Lido Deck. Would all women aboard kindly report to the library on the Promenade Deck. Again, this instruction applies to both crew and passengers. Please report immediately. *The Water Lily* is not in any danger, but it is imperative that we conduct a thorough and complete headcount as soon as possible. My personal apologies for any inconvenience."

There was a final crackle then the speakers fell silent. A moment later, muted sounds of activity filled the air. Doors opened and closed, voices murmured in mild alarm and grumbling irritation. The handful of people aboard the ship were making their way to the assigned locations to comply with the Captain's order.

Elli turned toward Sasha. "Should we go?"

"I can't. I'm the one they're looking for. It would be suicide for me to walk into the library."

"What about me?"

Sasha thought. "You should. You'll be safer if you do as they say. I can't guarantee your safety if you stay with me. And if you stay here and they sweep the rooms ..." She trailed off. Elli had seen the guns; she could fill in the blanks for herself.

Tears wobbled in Elli's eyes. "But what are you going to do?" she asked in a voice that cracked with fear.

Sasha smiled. "I'm a lot tougher than I look."

The other woman sniffled but smiled back. "I'm serious."

"So am I," Sasha told her with as much bravado as she could muster. "I'm going to wait until the two men split up. I assume one of them will head to the library."

"And the other to the tiki bar?" Elli guessed.

"No. That's probably just a ruse to get the men to one of the highest decks, where they'll be out of the way. I'll bet they know Connelly's not on the ship. So they just want to get me off the ship without any interference from the crew or passengers. This headcount thing will keep everyone busy. That's why they want the women to go down to Deck Four—it's closer to their getaway route. One of them will be positioned near the library to grab me. The other will probably be down below, waiting to make their escape."

"Do you think Captain van Metier knows he's leading you into a trap?"

Did he? That was an excellent question. Sasha couldn't imagine that he'd sell out one of his passengers, even if it meant a quick resolution and the guaranteed safety of the rest. But, then, she guessed it really depended on what sort of lawyers had drafted the SOP he was following. She'd run into more than a few who would weigh the benefits against the costs and recommend giving her up in a heartbeat.

"I'm honestly not sure," she answered. "It doesn't matter, though, because I'm not about to walk into any traps." She patted Elli gently on the arm. "Go. I'll see you in a bit."

Elli gaped at her. "What are you going to do?"

"I'm going to beat the big stupid one to within an inch of his life."

27.

LEO DRAGGED ONE of the empty cages across the floor and jammed it under the doorknob while Thiha Bo and Binh watched wide-eyed. He didn't expect the cage to be an overly effective barricade, but, at a minimum, it would slow down anybody who tried to enter the room. And that would be enough.

He hurried back to Binh's cage and squatted beside it. "I have friends who want to bring Mina's killers to justice. I want that, too. I also want to help you—all of you. These conditions, they're not right. You don't belong in cages. You shouldn't be lashed and beaten and half-starved. The work you're doing is dangerous and hard. You should be paid for it."

Thiha Bo had told him that their pay, when they even got paid, went directly to the staffing agencies. No one had talked to him about the physical abuse, but he'd seen the scars and bruises with his own eyes.

"But what can you do?" Thiha Bo asked.

"I can stop Captain Vũ. And then you can go home. Or find work on a legitimate boat, with a captain who will pay you and provide food, medication, a safe environment—not this." He knew he was speaking too fast for Thiha Bo to keep up with the translation, but he felt an overriding sense of urgency. He had to say his piece now while he had the chance. He gripped the bars and meet Binh's gaze. "Do you want my help?"

There was no need for Thiha Bo to translate that sentence. "Yes." Binh's dark eyes burned into his. "Help Binh."

Halfway there.

Leo exhaled. "Okay, good. I'll help you. But *I* need *your* help."

Thiha Bo repeated the words in Vietnamese. Binh wrinkled his forehead in confusion.

"He wants to know how," Thiha Bo said. "I do, too."

Leo rubbed the area between his upper lip and nose and thought how best to explain things. "I'm something like a police officer in the United States. I have contacts who can arrest Captain Vũ." I *hope.* "I need some men to storm the bridge with me."

Fear sparked in Binh's eyes when Thiha Bo told him what Leo had said, but the caged man tightened his grasp on the bars of his cage with his hands still tied at the wrists, squeezing so hard that his knuckles turned white. "Binh will help," he said in English without hesitation.

"Are you sure?"

Thiha Bo translated, and Binh nodded yes. He was sure. His eyes burned with intensity. Leo searched the room for something, anything, he could use to break the rusty padlock on the cage. Thiha Bo coughed and reached into the folds of his oversized tan cotton shorts and produced a fillet knife.

Leo held out his hand, and Thiha Bo carefully placed the curved blade in his palm. Then Leo crouched and took the padlock in his left hand, inspecting it. It was a large lock but cheaply made. He searched the recesses of his memory for his long-ago training. There would be no need to bust it apart after all. It was a simple pin-and-tumbler set-up. Easy enough to pick. Finesse won out over brunt force.

He eased the tip of the blade into the keyhole, pressed up, and wiggled the knife until he felt the springs press back. Then he pushed upward, jiggling the blade from side to side. Despite the size of the lock, Leo was sure there was only a single pin inside. A state-of-the-art lock would be overkill on a rundown shipping boat in the middle of nowhere.

In fact, Leo thought, the padlock was probably unnecessary altogether. He could have simply placed Binh in the cage and shut the door. Given the dynamics on the boat, Leo doubted he'd have tried to get out.

He gave the blade another good twist and felt the cylinder inside the lock rotate. He kept turning and, *voila*, it swung open. Thiha Bo's mouth fell open in amazement, and Binh laughed in disbelief. Leo opened the door and gestured for Binh to raise his bound hands. Leo carefully sawed through the rope, and it fell to the floor. Binh stepped out into the room, arched his back and stretched, then rubbed his wrists. Leo would have liked to have given him a few moments to enjoy his freedom, but they didn't have the time to spare.

He turned to Thiha Bo and held up the knife. "Do you mind if I hang on to this for a bit?"

"Please, keep it." Thiha Bo swallowed. "I will help you, too."

Leo tucked it into his waistband and gave the Burmese man an approving smile. "Thank you. Are you two ready?"

They flashed twin looks of uncertainty. He spoke reassuringly, "Just follow my lead. Captain Vũ won't be expecting us. He'll be surprised and slow to react. How many men will he have with him?"

Thiha Bo thought. "Two, perhaps three." His tone made it clear that he was guessing.

"How many will be armed?"

"Armed? With guns?"

"Yes."

"Just the captain. Nobody has weapons, not even his second in command." Thiha Bo was on solid ground now—his voice grew stronger, more certain.

Of course, Leo thought. A tyrant like Vũ would fear an uprising with good reason.

"Good. I'll take care of Captain Vũ. You two handle anyone else who's hanging around."

Thiha Bo translated the instructions then asked a question. "What do you mean by handle?"

"That's up to you. If you can convince them to join us—or at least not to interfere—that's ideal. But if any of the crew gets inspired to try to defend your captain, I'll need you to try to hold them back or fight them off until I have Vũ under my control. Can you do that?"

Thiha Bo laughed gutturally. "I don't think many will join an insurrection. But I know no one will protect Captain Vũ."

Leo sincerely hoped Thiha Bo was right about that.

Binh, who seemed to have caught the tenor of the conversation, if not its specifics, spat on the floor. His face was dark and resolute.

Leo surveyed his ragtag backup detail one last time. "Let's go."

28.

SASHA WATCHED AS Elli turned the corner and began to make her way down to the library. Once she was out of sight, Sasha sneaked along the deck, duck walking low and hewing close to the ship's bulwark. People were trickling from all directions, and the real danger of being spotted was making her pulse skyrocket. She paused and took several deep breaths. She told herself that almost everyone would make a beeline for the elevator rather than the stairs. All she had to do was make it to the stairwell unseen. Just ten more yards.

She started inching forward again, ignoring the cramping that had started to burn along her thigh muscles. Another twelve feet and she'd be at the top of the stairs. She could see the landing now.

The sound of the elevator swooshing by on its way up to the Lido Deck filled her ears, and she pressed herself against the wall and froze, sweat beading at her hairline. She had no idea whether she was visible from within the glass-walled elevator car or if anyone was looking in her direction. She waited until the car passed and then raced forward, covering the remaining distance to the stairs as rapidly as she could.

Once she reached the stairs, she more or less threw herself down them, hanging on to the bannister and running at full speed down each set, across the landing, and to the next. She didn't stop until she reached the lowest deck. Away from passengers' eyes, this deck was purely utilitarian and devoid of opulent finishes. Neatly labeled compartments housed the main engines, generators, electrical systems, and mechanical systems behind steel doors. Enormous pipes snaked overhead in a tangle of colors. The floor hummed with energy.

She skulked around to the ship's stern. There, she leaned over the railing and surveyed the water on the starboard side first, on a hunch. The men were wearing wetsuits. If they had boarded from the port, the whole wetsuit thing wouldn't have been necessary. She spotted a pair of black wave runners or jet skis or whatever they were called bobbing in the waves in the shadow of the hull.

But how had they boarded the ship? She hoisted herself up, balanced her feet on the bottom rail, then hung over the top rail and scanned the side. No rope, no grappling hook, no makeshift ladder. Nothing that suggested a way onto the boat.

Weird.

Well, she'd have plenty of time to puzzle over it while she waited for Mr. Big, Dumb, and Angry to make his way down to the deck. Now, her priority was to find a spot to lie in wait. She walked a few paces until she found a suitable architectural column then settled into place behind it.

~ ~ ~ ~ ~ ~ ~ ~ ~ ~

Leo raised his left hand in a fist, almost as if he were about to knock on the door to the pilot room. Instead he turned his head and looked first at Binh, who was just a few steps behind him, and then Thiha Bo, who stood near the far end of the short corridor, ready to invent a distraction if someone walked up behind them. He raised his index finger, then his middle, and finally his ring finger to give them the count.

One, two, three.

He turned to his right and shouldered the door open with his full weight. As he rammed it open, the wood cracked and splintered. He kept on going, letting his momentum carry him into the room, and went straight for the captain.

There was no doubt which man was Vū. He wore a filthy white captain's hat, and his lined, weathered face was hard and rat-like. On either side of him stood a barefoot man dressed in tattered shorts. His officers, apparently. They didn't look as though they received any easier treatment than did the crew and, true to Thiha Bo's prediction, they didn't seem inclined to get involved. They stood, hands at their sides, and stared at Leo.

Captain Vū, meanwhile, had grabbed his radio and was shouting into it. Leo couldn't make out the words, but it was clear from the tone that he was making an S-O-S call. He stepped forward and slapped the radio out of Vū's hand. It bounced off the instrument panel and dangled by its cord upside down.

Vū's face contorted into a mask of rage. He reached his hand into his right pocket, keeping his eyes on Leo.

Leo took another step forward. Now he was nose to nose with the captain. He grabbed the back of Vũ's head with his left hand and jammed the fillet knife under Vũ's chin.

"No." He repeated it in Vietnamese. "*Không.*"

Vũ froze, his hand still in his pocket.

"Thiha Bo!" Leo shouted without turning around.

"Yes?" He entered the room meekly.

"Tell Captain Vũ that if he takes his gun out of his pocket, I'll slit his throat before he even has a chance to pull the trigger."

Thiha Bo nodded and translated. He must have sounded convincing because Captain Vũ slowly removed his hand. He held it out toward Leo to show that it was empty. Leo kept the knife pressed on the man's throat and used his left hand to fish the gun out of the man's pocket.

Vũ's officers exchanged a look. The one standing to the left of the captain cleared his throat and said something to Thiha Bo. The other one took off and tried to skitter out of the room. Binh stepped into his path to block him.

"What did he say?" Leo asked. He jerked his head to the one who hadn't run.

"He asked if you're going to kill them."

Leo let his eyes travel over the two officers. "Should I?"

Thiha Bo shook his head wildly. "No. They're weak and foolish. They only served the captain out of fear."

"They've probably made some enemies among the crew. Tell them they can go but they should keep a low profile. I wouldn't be surprised if some of the men want to settle old scores."

Thiha Bo repeated the instruction, the officers bobbed their heads in understanding, and Binh moved aside. The men raced out of the room.

"Could you bring me the rope?" Leo said.

Thiha Bo stepped forward with a length of fishing rope.

"Tie him up, please," Leo instructed, stepping to his right so that Thiha Bo could do so. He continued to hold the knife against Vũ's throat.

Thiha Bo fastened a tight, expert knot around the captain's wrists and held on to the end of the rope. He looked at Leo with an expectant expression.

"Good. Now he goes in one of his own cages. Let Binh do the honors. I need you to help me place a radio call to the American embassy in Bangkok. And then you can explain to the others what's happening."

Thiha Bo handed the rope to Binh, and Leo returned Thiha Bo's fillet knife. Binh led his prisoner out of the room.

Leo examined the captain's compact Smith & Wesson 9-millimeter. As a rule, the only gun he trusted was his gun. This one, he distrusted in particular. He hit the magazine release, cleared the cartridge from the chamber, and locked the slide open. If the captain's weapon maintenance was anything like the care and attention he afforded his vessel and crew, Leo figured the gun hadn't been cleaned, oiled, or checked in years, maybe decades. The last thing he needed was to shoot himself in the thigh because the recoil spring was bad or the thing jammed from years of storage in humid conditions. He slid the cartridge into his pocket and rested the unloaded weapon on the top of the instrument panel. Then he turned his attention to the radio.

~ ~ ~ ~ ~ ~ ~ ~ ~ ~

Sasha shifted her weight from one leg to the other. The space she'd squeezed into between the column and the ship's wall was tight, but she had to stay loose and keep her muscles warmed up so she was ready to pounce as soon as she saw the big guy.

If she ever saw the big guy.

She'd been certain she'd predicted the men's plan. It was the only logical strategy. And they clearly weren't amateurs. But as the minutes ticked by, she began to have doubts. Maybe the thin guy had sent the big one to the library and was busy checking all the empty rooms for her. Or maybe they hadn't split up at all and would come down here together eventually. Which would be an unfortunate development. Or maybe—

Her worrying was interrupted by the sound of someone clanging down the steps. Someone heavy-footed. She risked a peek around the column and couldn't suppress a grin. There he was, right on cue.

She exhaled and ran through the steps she'd sketched out: wait until he walked over to the railing to check on the watercraft vehicles. He'd undoubtedly check to make sure they were still anchored. It was human nature. And when he did, she'd rush him from behind while he was bent over, looking down into the water. This was the riskiest part of the maneuver for the simple reason that her Krav Maga instructor taught self-defense, not attacks. She didn't have a fluid, well-ingrained attack sequence to spring on the man.

But, she reasoned, it hardly mattered. Once she hit him, he'd strike back. And then she'd be on more familiar ground. Striking first was still the smart play. It would surprise him, throw him off balance, and give her the upper hand from the very beginning. She shook out her hands and rolled her neck from side to side.

His feet hit the deck with a thud. She peered out from behind the support. After a glance in each direction, he headed straight for the railing. She tensed, ready to pounce.

He was approximately five feet away from the edge of the ship when a ringtone sounded from inside the small waterproof sack slung over his back. He stopped, unzipped the back, dug out a mobile phone encased in a rugged cover, and answered the call.

"Ye-ah?" His voice gave him away as an American, and he spoke with a distinct twang of a Southern accent. He listened for a moment, frowning.

"What'd ya' mean there's a disturbance? What do they want us to do about it now—I thought we're supposed to get the girl?" He waved his arm like an angry gorilla while he spoke.

The caller must have tried to further explain because he fell silent again. Then he shrugged.

"Whatever. It's Thale's dime. Did she show up in the library?"

A pause and then a snort. "Naw, that's fine. I'll go. How hard can it be to quell a rebellion of half-starved sea slaves? You stay here and grab the woman. I'll take care of Vū's crew. Hell, in a couple hours' work, we can manage a double payday, my brother."

He laughed and slapped his thigh in excitement. Then he stowed his phone and removed a set of suction cups from the pouch. Sasha watched intently as he lowered himself over the railing and disappeared from view.

She considered what she'd heard and recalculated her odds. Now there was only one armed man to contend with, but she was without a weapon. Part of the point of jumping the cowboy was to wrest control of his gun. She might not know how or be willing to use it, but his partner wouldn't have known it.

Now what?

It was time for another plan. She waited until she heard the PWC's engine roar to life in the water below and then slipped out from behind the column.

29.

AN VAN METIER could no longer ignore his latest headache. This one had been building behind his temples from the moment he'd arrived back on *The Water Lily*. Currently, he felt as though his head were screwed firmly into a vise, which was being twisted ever so slowly.

He grimaced at his visitor and palmed a handful of pain relievers from the bottle. The presence of Thale's hired guns was assuredly not helping matters. Nor was the fact that the blasted Connelly woman remained unaccounted for. Add in the utter public relations nightmare of passengers and crew being corralled for an indeterminate length of time under the guise of a headcount, and it all amounted to a mess. He took a swig of water to wash down the pills then wiped his mouth.

"What do you propose we do?" he asked the man, Derek Something or Other, who was standing in the middle of the control room in his glossy black wetsuit with a gun dangling from his right hand.

Derek's expression dripped with disdain. "What're you asking me for? My job was to board the ship, snatch up the woman, and get off fast. No fuss, no muss. Your job was to make her available. I've been cooling my heels waiting for her to turn up in your library, but she hasn't. So where is she?"

Where, indeed? How was it possible for a single person—and an exceedingly small one, at that—to cause so much trouble?

He sighed. "I wish I knew."

"Wishes are for losers, captain. What this calls for is action."

Jan studied the man's craggy face. He looked like a man with a plan, and that worried Jan. "What sort of action?"

Derek raised an eyebrow. "I'm going to sweep this ship top to bottom, shooting everyone who hasn't reported to the tiki bar or the library, as ordered. How's that sound?"

Jan's mouth went dry but he barked out a response nonetheless. "That's unacceptable." He knew better than to plead with this man or to try to reason with him. He'd encountered Derek's type before—in the navy. Blood-thirsty loose cannons looking for action. The only way to keep them in line was to remind them of the hierarchy. He may not have direct command over the mercenary, but he *was* the captain of *The Water Lily*. This was his ship, and there would be no mayhem and carnage on his watch.

Derek waited.

"We can't keep the passengers holed up drinking cocktails and submitting to a manufactured head count forever. I'll help you find the Connelly woman myself and deliver her to you and your partner. Where is he, by the way?" He needed to keep tabs on these two. He couldn't have armed men patrolling the cruise ship willy-nilly. They were liable to bump into the ship's security officers, who were already asking uncomfortable questions about the headcount.

"Something came up. He was called away to handle another matter. I'm confident I can handle one woman by myself." He smirked.

"The evidence suggests otherwise." Jan gave him a long look, then pressed the power button on the row of monitors that were tied to the ship's closed-circuit camera system. The screens flickered to life. He scanned them, sector by sector, then pointed to a screen in the middle row. "There, she's on the bottom deck, just outside the engine room. And judging by the life vest she's wearing, I'd say she's not planning to stay long."

Derek was already halfway out of the room. Jan overrode the security program to interrupt the recording. There was no need to have video of what was about to happen to Mrs. Connelly. He leaned back in his chair and closed his eyes. He'd give Derek another ten minutes to do his work, then he'd instruct the staff to begin releasing the passengers.

~ ~ ~ ~ ~ ~ ~ ~ ~ ~

Sasha eased her right leg over the ship's edge and sat straddling the railing. She peered down. The water seemed a long way away. And she didn't have a set of suction cups handy. She did, however, have a child-sized life jacket that she'd found in a box full of emergency equipment. And she had two flares jammed in her pocket of her sundress. Still, this idea seemed to be questionable at best.

But when she examined her situation from a dispassionate point of view, her self-defense training told her to get off the ship.

Here goes nothing.

She swung her other leg over the bar and balanced atop the railing, gripping it with both hands and took a long breath. She couldn't judge exactly how many feet she was about to jump. She could only hope she didn't break any bones that would make getting to shore impossible. She removed her hands from the railing and leaned forward and—

Suddenly, she was falling. Not forward, over the railing and toward the sea. But backward, her arms flailing as she toppled toward the deck. She twisted her head and felt a sharp yank at the base of her head, where her ponytail was secured.

She wasn't falling. She was being pulled by her hair.

A flash of black registered in her line of sight. By the time she realized it was the man in the wetsuit, her back was hitting the deck.

Get up, get up, get up. Move.

Her brain screamed the instruction, and her muscles twitched, eager to comply. The worst thing she could do would be to land flat on her back. That would enable the man to straddle her, control her arms, and overpower her.

Winded and already aching from the force of the impact with the deck, Sasha obeyed her brain and body's signals and immediately rolled to her left side, coming to rest on her hip.

Constant movement, she reminded herself, grateful that she and Daniel had been working on the principle of continuous combat motion in the studio.

The man lurched forward, looming over her, trying to plant his knees on the deck on either side of her while she bucked. She folded her right leg and jammed her shin and kneecap up against his stomach. She pressed her left heel against his right thigh.

As she lifted her leg, the flares fell out of her pocket and rolled along the deck, out of reach. Not that they were going to be much use in a ground fight, but they were the closest thing to a weapon she had. And now they were gone.

Focus, she scolded herself.

The man grinned down at her, as if he found her struggling to be mildly amusing or, worse yet, cute. Anger flared in her belly. Unable to straddle her, he brought his right arm up and back, open-handed. She realized he wasn't planning to punch her. He was either going to slap her or grab her by the throat—and she didn't intend to find out which it was.

She pulled back her left leg, flexed her foot, and landed a heel kick to the underside of his chin, right at the base of his jawbone. His neck bobbled and his head whipped back as her heel connected and the shock rippled up his jawbone to his brain.

If she'd been standing, she might have delivered the kick with enough force to knock him out. But she wasn't standing; she was kicking from the ground. At best he'd be stunned and numb-faced for a few moments. She had to hurry.

She crabbed backwards on her elbows a few paces to get out from under him then scrabbled to her feet. He was still on his knees, already reaching around for his backpack—and, no doubt, his gun.

She stretched out her hand and snatched at the backpack straps. She jerked down hard, with all her might. He wobbled forward, but swatted her hand away. The bag stayed secured on his shoulders. She wasn't going to be able to access the gun.

Time for the second-best option: ensure he couldn't get to it either. As he pushed himself to his feet, she turned and aimed her right elbow at his midsection, right in his gut, then followed with a punch from her left hand. He doubled over and braced his hands on his knees for a moment, then raised his head, enraged.

He slammed into her, but she pivoted to the side. She evaded the full force of his weight, but even the glancing blow to her hip sent her flying off-balance. She hit a metal box built into the deck wall hard enough that it knocked the wind out of her.

He was strong. And pissed. And he was coming at her again.

He loomed over her. Then he grabbed her and pulled her to her feet in a tight bear hug. She went ragdoll limp and sagged into him. Her face was pressed against the fleshy underside of his arm— she could feel it through his neoprene wetsuit. She hinged her jaw, opened her mouth wide, and bit down hard.

He yelped and tried to pull away. She clamped her mouth shut and held on tight, like Mocha and his favorite chew toy.

He cursed and wriggled.

She bit harder. He used his free arm to push at her jaw, forcing her face away from his armpit.

This was her chance. She reached out blindly and yanked, pulling the backpack down over his shoulders. It landed on the deck between them.

They both lunged for it, but she was faster. She grabbed it and hefted it over her head then threw it, two-handed, over the railing and into the water.

She planted her feet in a fighting stance and raised her hands. Now that his handgun was on its descent to the bottom of the ocean, along with his suction cup system and, presumably, the key to his watercraft, she was ready for a real fight.

"Let's see what a big man you are without your toys," she taunted him.

His eyes narrowed to twin black pinholes. He didn't waste any time. His fist came out of nowhere, and he aimed an explosive right cross at her face. She jerked her head to the side and evaded a straight hit. But his fist still caught the edge of her cheekbone.

The pain radiated out from her cheek and covered the entire side of her face. He punched again but she deflected the blow with her right forearm. She continued to slide her blocking arm forward and raked her fingers across his eyeballs, gouging them.

He screamed and clawed at her arm with both hands. She used the opening to throat punch him with her stronger left fist. His face contorted in rage and he reached out to choke her. As his hands closed around her throat, she launched a straight front kick, driving her right foot straight into his groin. He huffed out in pain and curved his body inward. She used her momentum from the kick to pivot and smash her right elbow into his ribs. She heard the crack of bone splintering, and he inhaled sharply.

"Ms. McCandless-Connelly, may I be of assistance?" A polished, accented voice called from the stairs, just as she was preparing to finish off her assailant.

She didn't remove her eyes from the man, but he glanced toward the stairwell and his eyes widened. He froze.

Sasha flicked her eyes toward the stairs and nearly fell over at the sight of Bruce, her buttoned-up butler, training what had to be a harpoon gun on the man in the wetsuit. Behind him, several of the ship's uniformed security officers clattered down the stairs.

Sasha let out a long, shaky breath. She stared at the gunman with blazing eyes. "You're lucky they're here."

He didn't respond as two security officers hoisted him by the arms, expertly snapped a set of handcuffs around his wrists, and dragged him toward the stairs.

"Are you quite all right, Ms. McCandless-Connelly?" Bruce asked.

She took a quick inventory. Aside from some aches and a handful of bruises that were already forming, she'd be fine. She pressed her cheekbone gingerly in the spot where the man had landed his first punch. It was tender, but the bone seemed to be intact. At worst, she'd have a shiner in the morning.

"I could use a cup of coffee," she cracked.

"Respectfully, I think a nice chamomile tea might be a better choice," Bruce shot back.

Elli's voice drifted down from the landing. "Oh, bother. This calls for the hard stuff. Let's get you cleaned up, then we'll have a couple of nice, stiff Hendricks and tonics."

Sasha curved her mouth into a grin and felt something stuck in her teeth. She used two fingers to remove what appeared to be a scrap of wetsuit fabric. *Nice.*

She almost giggled at the absurdity of the situation, but then she remembered that Connelly was still unaccounted for, and the laughter died in her throat.

30.

LEO YAWNED. It wasn't because he was bored or even tired. Rather, in the aftermath of the confrontation with the captain, the adrenaline that had flooded his body drained just as quickly, and he crashed. Now, having contacted Mel and read her the coordinates off the boat's instrument panel, all there really was left to do was wait. Wait and worry about Sasha.

Mel had filled him in on Ron's decision to send her back to The Water Lily. He understood the legat's reasoning, but he also knew it would be driving Sasha insane to be sidelined on the cruise ship with no idea where he was or what Mel was doing to track down Mina's killers. And a sidelined

Sasha was apt to get herself into trouble. He'd just have to trust that Sasha was keeping herself busy with a good book or a spa treatment for a few more hours. As soon as Mel and the authorities arrived to arrest Vũ and free the crew, he'd hitch a ride back to the cruise ship.

"Sir?" Thiha Bo poked his head into the cabin.

"Please, it's Leo."

"Leo, can you come talk to the men? They have a lot of questions about what will happen to them."

To be honest, he didn't have any answers— other than the obvious one: they were about to win their freedom.

"Okay, sure," he agreed. He needed to stretch his legs. Plus, it would give him an excuse to check in on Binh, who was guarding Captain Vũ.

He stood up, and the gun he'd placed on the instrument panel caught his eye. It was better not to leave that laying out in the open—just in case. He instinctively slipped it into his pocket before trailing Thiha Bo out of the room.

He stepped out onto the deck and filled his lungs with salty sea air. Despite the circumstances, he had to admire the otherworldly beauty of his surroundings. The sun, low and about to set, was a golden fireball that lit the deep blue water. He took a long look, searing it into his memory, wishing he was sharing the view with Sasha, and then turned back to the ship.

Thiha Bo stood at his shoulder, ready to translate his words into the handful of languages that would hold meaning for the assembled men who were staring at him with a mixture of expectant and frightened expressions—maybe even the occasional glimmer of hope.

Hope made him think of Binh. He turned to Thiha Bo. "I'm going to go get Binh. He should be here for this. Tell them to wait a minute."

Thiha Bo nodded his understanding and began to speak to the men. Leo ducked under the mast and started toward Vũ's private quarters.

He was halfway down the hallway when he heard the roar of a motor approaching.

Mel. She'd made great time; this was much sooner than he'd thought she'd arrive.

He detoured to the aft, toward the noise, to greet her.

But, it wasn't Mel with a cadre of police officers and FBI agents dropping anchor. Instead, a beefy white guy, with thinning blond hair and a sunburnt neck, had brought a personal watercraft to a stop near the boat and was climbing the rigging one-handed, a snub-nosed revolver in his right hand.

Leo snorted in irritation. This yahoo was clearly not one of the good guys. In fact, if he were a betting man he'd guess that the wetsuit-clad gunman was one of Thale's so-called soldiers.

He was in no mood for a protracted struggle. "Binh!" he called, projecting his voice toward the captain's quarters.

After a moment, Binh's face appeared in the doorway. He was wide-eyed.

Leo gestured for him to come join him. Binh glanced back, no doubt to ensure that his prisoner was secured. Leo wished he had the vocabulary to tell him that Captain Vū wasn't going anywhere. But Binh must have come to that conclusion on his own because he pulled the door firmly shut and hustled down the corridor.

Leo put a hand on the Vietnamese man's shoulder and directed his attention to the man who was in the process of hoisting himself up onto the deck.

"Is that one of the men who killed Mina? One of the soldiers?"

Leo hoped Binh would be able to follow the gist of what he was saying. Whether he understood the question or not turned out to be irrelevant. Binh's entire body went rigid and the veins in his neck throbbed as he stared unblinkingly at the man. That was all the answer Leo needed.

He patted Binh on the arm. "Stay here," he whispered.

Then he walked purposefully toward the intruder, reaching into his pockets as he did so. Without missing a step, he loaded the magazine into the gun, chambered a round, and raised the weapon.

He skipped the preamble and aimed the Smith & Wesson just below the man's right shoulder. He steadied his hand and fired.

The blond man jerked his arm and released his gun, which hit the deck with a thud. Then he grabbed his shoulder with his left hand and fell back into the water with a splash.

"What the—?" the man shouted.

Leo walked over to the edge of the boat and pointed the gun down toward him. "Good, you speak English. I hope you understand it, too. Now shut your mouth or I'll do you like you did Mina."

The man screwed up his face in confusion.

"The woman you shot had a name, genius. It was Mina."

Comprehension lit in the man's eyes, and fear mingled with the pain that was etched on his face.

Leo turned to Thiha Bo, who had come out to see what all the noise was about. "Have someone fish him out, please. And put him in the cage next to the captain."

He hoped Mel got here sooner rather than later.
He was running out of cages.

31.

"ON BEHALF OF *The Water Lily* and, indeed, the entire Sacred Lotus family, I extend our profuse apology for what you've endured, Ms. McCandless-Connelly."

Sasha arched a brow at the name. So all it took for Captain van Metier to use her actual legal name was an attempted abduction? Nice to know.

Despite his flowery, overly formal apology, the captain looked as though he were sucking on something exceedingly sour. And he was sweating. And his eyes were flitting all around the medical center.

She realized Captain van Metier was waiting for her to say something in response to his speech. "Okay," she said dully.

The captain exchanged worried looks with Julia, who was hovering near the spare cot against the wall. The hostess stepped forward and kneeled beside Sasha's chair.

"Ms. McCandless-Connelly, we're just beside ourselves about this ... horrifying incident. Please, what can we do for you?"

"Well, for one thing you can explain why the ship's response to being boarded by armed men was to round up the passengers like sitting ducks instead of deploying the security unit to handle the attackers."

Julia jerked her head toward Captain van Metier. "I don't think it's my place to answer that, Captain?"

He pushed back his shoulders. "I personally encountered the men on one of the upper decks. I was alone and unarmed; they, as you know, had weapons. In my judgment, the safest course of action was to accede to their initial demand. Your experience was regrettable, I don't deny that. But, by the same token, no one was killed or abducted. So I stand behind my actions."

Sasha stared at him. He did seem to be at peace with what happened. That made one of them.

"Ms. McCandless-Connelly, are you sure there's nothing you need?" Julia asked. Her tone was warm and soft and undeniably upset.

Sasha looked into the hostess's troubled eyes and relented. She could believe Julia was genuinely concerned about her, and not just because of the possibility of a negligence lawsuit.

"I'm okay. Truly. What I'd really like is for someone to track down my husband on the mainland." Her voice caught in her throat.

"Of course," Julia said. And without asking any questions as to how she was supposed to find him, she slipped out the door in a rustle of silk.

A flustered Dr. Harmon piped up, "Are you sure you won't take a sedative, Ms. McCandless-Connelly?"

"I'm sure." She considered suggesting he offer one of his pills to the ship's captain, who looked like he could benefit from one.

"I'm ready to go now," Sasha said, looking at Dr. Harmon, although she was really addressing the captain. She pushed herself out of the chair.

"Please rest. You've been through a terrible ordeal," the doctor intoned.

"I'll escort you to your room," Captain van Metier said in a voice that made clear the issue wasn't up for discussion.

That was the last thing she wanted.

"I don't think—"

"I'm afraid I must insist. Your embassy will be wanting a statement from you, and I'll need to make the necessary arrangements. So we really should speak about your availability."

At the mention of the U.S. Embassy, Sasha's mood brightened. If she could get in touch with Mel, she might be able to get an update on Connelly and the fishing boat.

"I understand," she said. As they stepped out into the corridor, she tensed reflexively. "Where's the man who attacked me? Is he still on the ship?"

Captain van Metier shook his head no. "We've handed him over to the local police. He's in the Laem Chabang jail. He can't bother you, I assure you. With any luck, you'll never have to lay eyes on him again."

Her lawyer-brain wondered if that could possibly true, but given that she knew less than nothing about Thai criminal procedure, she simply nodded. "That would be nice. I'm ready to have a conversation with the people at the embassy now," she told him.

His face tightened. "That's not typically how this works. I'll need to go through the proper channels at The Sacred Lotus, and they'll interface with the ambassador's people. The diplomatic dancing will take some time. And we'll need to give them your schedule going forward."

He was watching her face closely while he spoke, and she got the distinct impression he was trying to gauge her reaction. *Creepy.* The skin on her arms felt as if it if were crawling. *Oh, stop it*, she chided herself. You don't like the man, and he *is* an insufferable prig; but, this is his ship and he's probably in a near-panic over what happened today despite his refusal to admit it.

She gave him a tired smiled. "That's fine, too. I'll be sure to provide my contact information to Julia or Bruce so the authorities can take a statement from me when they're ready." They reached the hallway to her room and she stifled a yawn. "Now, if you'll excuse me ..."

"Of course. Don't hesitate to call for me if you should need anything." He bowed stiffly. She walked away from him as fast as she could, eager to get back to her suite and away from his penetrating stare.

~ ~ ~ ~ ~ ~ ~ ~ ~ ~

Jan van Metier held his breath as he watched Sasha Connelly try the door to her room without running her key card past the reader—testing it, to ensure that it was locked. It was. She waved her keycard at the small red eye, waited a moment, then opened the door, and walked into the room. Her desire to check the lock was an understandable impulse in light of the attack, but also one that could have gone badly for him. He'd remembered to reactivate her locks after that idiot Derek had let her get the best of him. But until he witnessed her unlocking the door, he hadn't been entirely sure the reactivation had worked.

He breathed out slowly. That was one worry to tick off his outsized list of vulnerabilities. There remained plenty of areas of danger, he well knew. He would have to manage the Connelly woman's interactions with her embassy, for one. For another, he'd have to stay apprised of the Thai authorities' investigation into the botched abduction. Thale had assured him the man was a professional and would maintain his silence. He had to trust that confidentiality would extend to him, as well as to Thale. His contact at Thale failed to mention that it kept key local law enforcement personnel on its payroll, but he knew that to be the case from personal experience. On balance, he felt that his exposure was limited.

He was somewhat concerned that, as word spread among the passengers about the tussle between Mrs. Connelly and the gunman, there'd be some alarm about the ship's safety. But he'd already decided that he'd insinuate that Mrs. Connelly was to blame for what happened to her. If she'd simply reported to the library as instructed, she wouldn't have been accosted. He imagined that would be enough to quell any concerns.

Still, he would feel better about everything once they were out of Thai waters. The stress and strain of the situation was making him antsy; he craved the release that came from chasing the dragon. But he knew this was not the time for indulgence. Discipline and rigor would see him through—and once the passengers disembarked in Ho Chi Minh City, he would reward himself with a visit to his favorite Vietnamese heroin purveyor.

Steady, Jan, he told himself. *Keep a steady hand, and you will sail right through this storm.*

32.

EO HAD JUST checked on his prisoners for the zillionth time when Binh came running up the hallway and tugged on Leo's shirtsleeve. He followed Binh along the corridor to the stern of the ship. Binh pointed. A police speedboat was zipping across the waves toward them, followed by a second vessel. At last, reinforcements were coming.

He turned to Binh. "It's okay. They're going to help us." He had to trust his tone would convey his message even if his words were meaningless.

The panic in Binh's eyes remained. Several crew members ran past them, gesturing toward the boats and shouting at one another. He realized that after the shooting, he'd never addressed the men. People had scattered during the excitement, and his focus had been elsewhere. Now he was going to regret it.

Frustrated, Leo set off to look for Thiha Bo. He found him manning the instrument panel, ensuring that the boat didn't drift off course.

"The police are coming," Thiha Bo remarked.

"Right, and the men have spotted the boats. We never talked to them about what to expect. I'm afraid they're going to panic."

"Yes," Thiha Bo agreed. "The men will be scared. Most of us don't have the proper paperwork. Some of us may have legal problems back home."

The man's voice was steady, but something about his words made Leo search his face. "Do you have legal problems?"

He swallowed. "I owe a debt I cannot pay." He lowered his eyes to the floor.

Leo exhaled. "I'll explain the situation to the authorities, but I need you to help me calm everyone down. I'm afraid someone's going to do something really stupid."

"Such as dive overboard despite not knowing how to swim?" Thiha Bo asked, pointing to a thin Cambodian who was poised on the prow, prepared to do exactly that.

Leo raced out and pulled him back onto the deck while the Burmese man hurriedly made the rounds from group to group assuring them in several languages that they were safe. The haunted looks the crew members gave him made clear they didn't fully believe Thiha Bo's claims. They just needed to have a little faith, Leo told himself. As soon as Mel and the police boarded, their trust would pay off.

The lead boat pulled up close and two police officers fashioned a two-by-four into a temporary ramp leading up to the deck of the fishing boat. They gave Mel a boost and allowed her to board first, followed by a tall, stooped man who was clearly a Westerner—he had to be Ron.

"Mel," Leo called, waving so she'd see him.

She walked straight toward him, grabbed him by the shoulders, and whispered, "I'm sorry about how this is going to go down. Just trust me. It'll work out."

He was still processing her words, which sounded eerily like the ones he'd spoken to the crew, when she turned and shouted to Ron, "I'll secure the prisoner."

The prisoner? It took Leo a moment to realize she was talking about him, but at about the time the metal handcuffs clinked shut around his wrists, it all fell into place. He studied her, but her face was a blank mask.

She'd asked him to trust her. It didn't seem as though there were another choice, so he cleared his throat and said, "There's a handgun in my right front pocket. It's locked and loaded."

Her eyes sparked. "Thanks," she said in a low voice before she slid her hand into his pocket and retrieved the gun. "Take a seat." She pushed down on his shoulder gently and he lowered himself to a wooden chest that was pushed up against the starboard wall.

He sat and watched in dismay as the Thai police streamed onto the boat and swarmed the men, cuffing them to several long lengths of chain. An officer paraded a line of men past him, and he saw tears shining in Binh's eyes. He looked away.

~ ~ ~ ~ ~ ~ ~ ~ ~ ~ ~

Binh tried to focus on staying calm. He breathed in through his nose, out through his mouth, clearing his mind of all the chatter that threatened to break him. He was bound at the wrists, but this time not by a piece of fishing rope. Gleaming metal bracelets connected by a loop to a long chain hung from his hands. Uniformed officers shouted in rapid-fire Thai. Although he didn't recognize all the words they yelled, he knew they were demanding papers, proof that the crew had migrated properly and were working legally on the boat. He also knew that no one in the line of shackled men had such documents.

Just breathe.

When the officers reached him, he raised his eyes and met their stares but could not find any words. They moved on. The man in front of him, a Thai national, responded to their questions with an answer that repeatedly invoked Captain Vũ's name.

It hardly mattered though. No matter what happened now to Captain Vũ or the white man in the second cage, Mina's killer, this was the end of the road for Binh. He had no money to bribe the police. He would go to prison and shame his family. He lowered his head and closed his eyes.

33.

LEO SAT ON rickety rattan chair that Mel had produced from the bowels of the ship and stared unyieldingly at Ron, the lead legal attaché to the United States Embassy in Bangkok. Ron stared back. Mel cleared her throat uneasily, her eyes darting around the empty captain's quarters. The cages had been removed, Vũ and the American taken somewhere—where, Leo didn't have a clue. Ron hadn't said a word, but Leo damned sure wasn't going to break the silence.

In the end, Mel spoke first. "Leo, you have to understand. There are optics involved."

He snorted. Of all the governmental buzzwords that gave him hives, *optics* was the worst of the entire rotten bunch. All it meant was that the speaker was advocating deception for the sake of appearance.

She pressed on, undaunted by his reaction. "It's true. This is a delicate balancing act. There are political considerations here."

"Such as?"

Ron spoke up. "Such as, you're an American national who just shot another American national on a fishing boat you're not supposed to be on."

"He killed a girl!"

"Allegedly."

Leo gritted his teeth. "If the jackboots out there would ask the men they're rounding up, at least two of them can corroborate it."

Mel put a hand up. "Hang on. You can relax about the crew."

"You want me to relax about the crew you've got handcuffed and who are being interrogated as to whether their papers are in order?"

"Yes. They're not going to be detained. Once they're identified, there's a representative from a seafarer's welfare organization out of Sriracha Harbour waiting in the speedboat to take them to the mariner's center." She huffed out an angry breath. "But, hey, go ahead and underestimate us."

"I'm sorry." He was; he should have trusted the legal attaché's office more than he had. "What's going to happen to them at this center?"

"It depends on where they're from, what kind of physical condition they're in, and what they want to do next," Ron said. "These folks at the NGOs are pros at navigating the social services and helping the mariners, okay? They'll get them set up with medical care, housing, that sort of thing. They're in good hands. They'll be better off than they were on this blasted boat—that much is for sure."

The tension drained out of Leo's body. "And what about me?"

Mel looked pointedly at Ron. Ron coughed into his fist.

"Ron?" Leo insisted.

"You're going to have to spend a night in the lockup."

"I'm going to Thai prison?" Leo hoped a clarification would prove him wrong.

"A holding cell, to be precise about it. Only for one night. Your ... er ... unofficial status is causing a bit of a problem. Homeland Security isn't letting us claim you as a contractor or an agent or anything else. You're strictly a civilian as far as the Royal Thailand Police are concerned. A civilian who shot a professional armed security guard retained by a Thai company. You see how it looks?"

He did see how it looked. But, prison? His throat felt dusty. "If that's the case, how can you be so sure it's just going to be an overnight?"

Mel and Ron exchanged another glance. "Officially, the Department of Justice isn't going to get involved. But Hank knows someone who knows someone. Money's going to exchange hands. It's just taking some time to get all the transfers ironed out. And the police need to be able to say they arrested you, otherwise it'll look bad."

Leo shook his head. This couldn't be happening. And, yet, it was.

"No good deed goes unpunished, huh?" Mel said gently.

"Something like that." His voice sounded gruff to his own ears. "Can I call Sasha?"

Yet another look passed between the legats before Ron answered, "I'm sorry, son. That one phone call thing isn't really the way it works here. And we have to hand you over now."

"I'll get in touch with Sasha," Mel promised.

~ ~ ~ ~ ~ ~ ~ ~ ~ ~ ~

"He's in prison?" Sasha repeated the words, bewildered. For a moment, she actually couldn't parse out the meaning of the phrase.

"Yes," Mel confirmed.

Sasha stared at the phone in her hand as if it must be malfunctioning, then she shook her head. "I don't understand what you're saying. Conn—Leo is *in prison?*"

Julia took an uncertain step forward, as if she regretted having gotten a call through to the embassy, after all, and wanted to wrest the phone out of Sasha's hands. Bruce placed a hand on the hostess's arm to stop her. Sasha ignored them both and focused her full attention on the phone in her hand. Maybe if she concentrated just a tiny bit harder, Mel's words would start to make sense.

"Yes. He's going to be okay. He's in isolation and we have a guard who's ... friendly ... assigned to him. In the morning, as soon as his paperwork is processed, Ron will personally bring him to the ship. Okay?"

No, it wasn't okay. Nothing about this was okay, she wanted to snap. But she bit down on her lip instead. She knew this wasn't Mel's fault. Lashing out at her lone ally in the country would be a mistake.

"Does he need a lawyer?" she asked. Finding a lawyer to represent her husband was something she could control, something she could *do* instead of sitting like a lump in a too-big, too-empty cruise ship suite while her husband cooled his heels in a jail cell.

"Not really. What he needs is the intervention of a good friend, and that's in the works. I promise."

Sasha deflated. "Okay. So I just, what, sit tight?"

"Yes, exactly. But now we need to talk about something else. The hostess from the cruise, the one who called the Embassy, said you were attacked."

"Oh, right." The entire episode with the guy in the wetsuit had faded from her mind, supplanted by the news that Connelly was in prison for commandeering a fishing boat and shooting some security guard.

"What happened?"

"I was sitting on the balcony outside a friend's room—a woman who hadn't gone ashore. We had a clear view of my suite, and we saw two men, Americans, dressed in black go storming into my room with guns in their hands."

"Two men?"

"Yeah. Not long after they came back out, Captain van Metier confronted them. They argued for a minute, but then he made an announcement telling the men to report to one location and the women to another."

"Did he say *The Water Lily* had been hijacked?"

Sasha tried to remember. "No. He said that it wasn't a safety exercise, but that he needed to do a headcount, urgently. I'm sure he was trying to avoid setting off a panic."

"Makes sense. Go on."

"My friend headed to the library, but I knew the men were looking for me, so I didn't go. Instead, I went down to the deck with the engine room and the mechanicals and stuff."

"Why?"

"Well, the men were both wearing wetsuits, so I figured they'd boarded from the starboard side. I wanted to see how they got on the boat."

"Wetsuits? Black wetsuits?"

"Well, yeah, they were black. Aren't most of them? Anyway, I looked over the edge and saw two black and red personal watercraft vehicles. I couldn't figure out how they'd scaled the hull, but later I saw one of them leaving. He had suction cups that he used."

"Why'd he leave?"

"They got a call. He said ... Oh, my gosh, he said he had to quell a rebellion on Captain Vũ's boat. That's ... that's where Connelly was?"

"Right. So, Austin Williams was on *The Water Lily* attempting to kidnap you when he was called away to Vũ's fishing boat, where your husband shot him."

Sasha couldn't seem to form words. "That's crazy," she finally managed.

"And his partner? Where's he now? He works with a guy named Derek McGraw."

"Well if Mr. McGraw is the guy who stayed behind, we had a ... um ... fight. He got the worst of it. He ended up in the brig, where he was held until the Laem Chabang police took him into custody."

"He's in the jail, right now?"

"As far as I know. Didn't van Metier give you a statement?"

"It was bare bones." Mel's tone suggested she wasn't too happy about it, either.

"This whole thing is giving me a headache. I don't like coincidences," Sasha said.

"Oh, there's no coincidence. McGraw and Williams are the men you saw murdering Mina this morning."

"Mel, I'm sorry. I'm crashing hard. I can't think straight. Can we talk tomorrow?" Sasha ended the call. She was drained and ready to collapse onto her bed.

Bruce and Julia whispered to one another for a moment and then stood, side by side, in the doorway to the sitting room eyeing her nervously.

"What?" she finally said.

Bruce began, "Ms. McCandless-Connelly—"

"You saved my life. I think we're on a first-name basis at this point."

"Sasha, then. Julia and I recommend that you not mention Mr. Connelly's current situation to anyone on the ship."

Her husband's imprisonment wasn't exactly the sort of news she'd want to spread far and wide anyway, but she couldn't stop herself from asking, "Why?"

"Captain van Metier is a bit of a stickler," Julia explained. "The legal attaché I spoke to, Ms. Anders, made it very clear that Mr. Connelly's incarceration is the result of a regrettable error that will be cleared up in short order. But, all the same, knowing the captain, he'll be very upset to hear that one of his passengers ended up on the wrong side of the law."

"Especially after today's event," Bruce added. "He detests any unusual activity that upsets the natural order of things. He's already beside himself that the ship was boarded and his passengers inconvenienced."

Sasha considered pointing out that her attack by a murderous mercenary was somewhat more troubling than an inconvenience, but she was suddenly too tired to argue. So, she simply said, "I understand. Now if you'll excuse me, it's quite late, and I'm exhausted."

They tripped over themselves in their hurry to leave her to get some rest. She chained and deadbolted the door behind them, doubled checked that it was locked, then triple checked.

And then, nineteen hours after she witnessed the callous murder of a teenaged girl; ten hours after she was stalked through the streets of Samut Prakan by a gunman; seven hours after she had a bare-knuckled fight with a mercenary; and ten minutes after learning that her husband was in a Thai prison cell, Sasha McCandless-Connelly ended her day the only way that made sense: she cried herself to sleep.

34.

J AN DIDN'T NEED to look at his titanium diver's watch to know that Leo Connelly had missed the final call to re-board *The Water Lily*, but he did it anyway. For effect. He pushed back his shirt cuff, squinted at the dial, and emitted a short, harsh sound of displeasure.

Beside him, Julia stiffened and clutched her clipboard to her chest.

"We don't depart for another two hours, sir. I'm sure he'll be here shortly."

He didn't turn to look at her as he spoke, but continued to stare straight ahead, out at the horizon. "Miss Otterbein, you know my rule."

His rule was elegant in its simplicity: Anyone not on *The Water Lily* by the designated time was left behind. He'd made exceptions in the past, of course. When the bus transporting passengers back from a Sacred Lotus-sponsored excursion in China had been delayed by an engine that had caught fire, he'd allowed the harried travelers to re-board late. When Mrs. Garner had experienced a mild cardiac infarction at the Singapore Art Museum, he'd permitted her to board after the medical center had made the necessary arrangements to transport her to the cruise center.

But exceptions were made at his discretion, after a careful consideration of the circumstances. And there were many situations in which he had refused to permit lollygaggers to board: inconsiderate honeymooners; flaky groups of older women who lost track of time at the markets; ineffective parents who failed to herd their offspring through a city's tourist attractions in a timely manner—all these hapless travelers had been left behind in ports of call throughout Asia. He had a schedule to keep. And those passengers who had managed to arrange their day properly should not be inconvenienced by those who had not.

Each of these points was true. Still, Jan could feel himself growing defensive. Sasha McCandless-

Connelly had been attacked on his ship. So far, he had no reason to believe that anyone suspected him of being complicit; after all, why would they? But if he were to leave behind the woman's husband one day later, how would that look? Appearances mattered.

He turned to Julia. "Where the devil is he, anyway? What sort of man doesn't return to his wife's side after the ordeal she's just lived through?"

Julia blinked at him wide-eyed, apparently struggling to craft a response. "I'm certain Mr. Connelly ... oh, look!" She used her pen as a pointer and traced the progress of a sleek black SUV that was slowly weaving through an area of the port in which motorized vehicles were prohibited. The car was headed directly toward their dock. Ordinarily, Jan would have radioed port security, but seeing as how a security vehicle was escorting the SUV, that step seemed superfluous.

An ice-cold wave of apprehension coursed through his body. Had the Thai authorities put it all together? Had Thale failed to pay a bribe? Maybe the American had rolled over, dishonoring his contractual vow of silence.

Stop that, he commanded himself. Whatever was about to happen, he would face it with the dignity that befit his position. He squared his shoulders and waited.

Julia and two of his petty officers descended the ramp and were standing at the bottom when the security golf cart and the SUV reached them. The port security officer executed a tight U-turn, gave a little wave of his hand, and headed back in the direction from which he'd come.

The driver of the SUV killed the engine and hopped out of the car. He was a stocky, olive-skinned man with short cropped hair. He wore a dark suit and mirrored sunglasses that hid his eyes. He walked around to the back of the car and opened the door.

A tall man, who held himself in the manner of someone who was accustomed to ducking under door frames and light fixtures, emerged. He was clearly a Westerner, judging by his coloring and his shock of wheat-colored hair. He, too, wore a suit and sunglasses. He turned back to the car and said something to someone still inside.

After a few seconds, a third man exited the car. Another tall man, but this one was broad-shouldered and stood erect. Jan couldn't make out his facial features—was he Asian or not? He had thick spiky hair and was dressed like a vacationer on holiday: a short-sleeved collared shirt, linen pants, and leather sandals. He glanced up toward *The Water Lily* and Jan got a good view of his face. Leo Connelly.

Mr. Connelly shook hands with the driver and then pointed toward Julia. He and the tall man approached the ramp where she stood. The three engaged in a few moments of animated conversation. Whatever they were saying to Julia elicited a series of gasps and fluttery hand gestures. Jan knew he could, and as a matter of decorum likely should, walk down the ramp to see what was going on.

But he stayed where he was. He was in a vulnerable position and maintaining the high ground felt safer to him. In any case, this was *his* ship; he was the captain. If the man wanted to speak to him, he could come to Jan. Apparently, that is what he wanted. He turned and called to the driver, who nodded and slid back into the car to wait. Then Julia, Mr. Connelly, and the tall man made their way up the ramp, trailed by the ship's officers.

Julia handled the introductions. "Captain van Metier, this gentleman is Ronald Rubin, the Legal Attaché to the United States Embassy in Bangkok. And, of course, you know Mr. Connelly."

Jan's stomach clenched. He ignored the tightness and smiled. "Mr. Rubin. Mr. Connelly."

"Call me Ron." The man from the embassy extended his hand.

Jan shook it firmly and ignored the request for informality. "What can I do for you, Mr. Rubin?"

"The American government wanted to ensure that this fine citizen was able to board the ship without incident. He was unavoidably delayed by an act of bravery and heroism that benefitted both the Royal Thai Government and the United States of America."

Jan flicked his gaze toward Mr. Connelly. The man seemed to be discomfited by the florid praise. He also appeared to be tired and somewhat disheveled. Jan looked back at the diplomat. "That sounds impressive."

"I assure you, it is. I'm not at liberty to speak about the details at the moment, but his actions were instrumental in securing the safety of several citizens from multiple nations. As a result, Mr. Connelly missed the final boarding time. I trust that's not a problem?" The man smiled.

"Certainly not. Mr. Connelly, in light of your service to your country and our host country, I would be honored if you and Mrs. Connelly would be my guests at my private table for dinner tonight," Jan said with all the sincerity he could muster.

A shadow flitted over Mr. Connelly's face but he wiped it away almost instantly. "That sounds great. Thank you. Now, if you'll excuse me ..." His voice was hoarse, and he was clearly eager to escape to his room.

"Of course." Jan nodded to Julia. "Have you scanned Mr. Connelly's keycard?"

"He's all set," Julia said in a warm voice.

Mr. Connelly turned toward the American official and clasped his arm. "Thanks for everything, Ron."

Rubin slapped him on the back in that jovial way the Americans had. "I'll be in touch. You take good care. Give Hank my best." Then he turned toward Jan and Julia. "Captain van Metier, Ms. Otterbein." He nodded and walked back down the ramp.

Jan turned to ask Mr. Connelly if he required an escort to his room, but he was already halfway to the elevator.

At his elbow, Julia mused aloud, "Isn't odd that both Mr. Connelly and Ms. McCandless-Connelly were each separately involved in some sort of drama at this port?"

It was odd, indeed, Jan thought darkly.

35.

ASHA SLEPT LIKE the dead and woke to the late-morning sunlight streaming through an opening in the drapes. She blinked in disbelief at the time displayed on the bedside clock then rolled over to nudge Connelly awake.

Her hand closed around a fistful of empty sheets and then she remembered. Connelly was in jail.

She sat up and pushed the hair out of her eyes. How could she have slept so well while her husband was stuck in some concrete cell, no doubt crawling with insects and who-knew-what? She was a terrible human being.

She stretched, and the muscles in her back protested in a fiery complaint. She got to her feet gingerly. She was sore all over. She ticked off the previous day's activities: five-mile run; evasive action in Samut Prakan; skulking around the cruise ship; oh, and, the hand-to-hand combat. She decided to give herself a pass on the good night's sleep. Her body had obviously needed it.

She padded to the glass doors, pulled the rod to open the drapes and let in the sun, and then began a series of gentle yoga postures to get herself moving. Next on the agenda would be some strong coffee.

And then? Then she'd raise holy hell until she got to speak to Connelly.

She was mid-cat in a cat-cow pose when she heard the doorknob jiggle. The chain did its job, and then there was light rapping at the door. Hopeful that it was Bruce with a breakfast tray, she abandoned the yoga in favor of sustenance and caffeine and trotted to the door. She grabbed a short silk robe off the back of one of the Queen Anne chairs and cinched it closed around her thin tank top and shorts.

She unlocked the deadbolt and slid off the chain then pulled open the door. "Bruce, just the man—"

Connelly stood in the doorway. He looked rumpled, tired, and gorgeous. He drank her in with his gray eyes for a long moment, then he gathered her into his arms, kicking the door closed with his foot.

"He better not be the man you were hoping to see," Connelly teased huskily before covering her mouth with hungry lips.

She wrapped her arms around his neck and arched her back to meet him. He was back. And in one very solid piece.

They fell onto the bed in a tangle of limbs. She trailed kisses from his jawbone to his shoulder. "Are you okay? Are you hurt?"

He shook his head. Then he took her chin in his hands and inspected her face. "Ron told me you were attacked. Did that dirtbag lay a finger on you?" He pushed the robe off her shoulders, searching her bare arms for bruises.

Some distant part of her logical brain informed her that this inventory of battle wounds was not normal foreplay, but she tucked the message away to deal with later.

"I'm okay. Just sore. Are you really okay?" she said, pulling his face down to hers.

"I'm better than okay." He smiled his crooked smile and then buried his face in her hair.

She wrapped her legs around his back and decided there were better ways to start one's day than with yoga and a cup of coffee.

~ ~ ~ ~ ~ ~ ~ ~ ~ ~

Sasha's mouth ached from smiling politely. Dinner at Captain van Metier's personal table reminded her of her entire 2-L summer of law school. It wasn't a fond memory.

Law firms offered summer associate positions to students who'd done well during their first two years of law school. The summer associates were paid obscenely well, coddled and pampered, and typically offered permanent employment at the end of the summer. Part of the law firm's goal during the summer was to impress its associates with mind-boggling displays of wealth and excess. Various partners had their own takes on what delivered that 'wow' factor.

Unfortunately for Sasha, her partner mentor had been a man not-so-affectionately nicknamed 'Attorney Peanut.' Although Reginald Bartholomew Bonaparte-Jones, Esquire, didn't *actually* have a monocle, top hat, and cane like the icon in the canned nuts commercial, he *did* have an extremely formal manner and had subjected her to endless, bland, overpriced dinners that stretched on for multiple courses and featured lengthy monologues by Attorney Peanut himself.

As Captain van Metier started his fourth consecutive story about his time in the Royal Netherlands Navy, she had to force her eyelids to stay open by sheer, wide-eyed will. It occurred to her that he hadn't asked her a single question—not about her family, not about her work, not about the U.S. presidential election. Bupkis. She glanced at the other end of the table where Connelly had totally lucked out and been seated next to Elli Kurck. Oliver was at the far opposite end, laughing and joking with an actor from a popular Mexican telenovela, who definitely told better stories than the captain.

"And so, you see, the ship was a *Karel Doorman* frigate, sometimes called an M-class, and—"

"That reminds me," Sasha interrupted, bored out of her mind and no longer concerned as to whether she was being rude, "what kind of ship is a dragon shuttle? Is that a military term or a fishing term or what?"

He pulled his head back like Java did when she smelled citrus—disgusted and perplexed all at once. "I beg your pardon?"

"A dragon shuttle. I heard someone use that term recently, and I thought it was a reference to a boat. It's very evocative, don't you think? I picture one of those Chinese paddle boats, but of course, that wouldn't be a shuttle. Anyway, I just thought you might know." She realized she was prattling, mainly because it was her first chance to speak in well over an hour—since just after the salads had been served and she asked the waiter for oil and vinegar dressing.

Captain van Metier was staring at her as if she'd taken off her dress and was dancing on the table. "I'm sure I don't have the slightest idea, Mrs. Connelly. Really, a dragon shuttle." He huffed and puffed and frowned and finally got up and walked away.

The older woman who was seated on the other side of the captain leaned across his empty seat and said, "What did you say to get his knickers in a twist?"

"I honestly don't know," Sasha told her.

"Well, I wish you'd have said it sooner. I finally had to turn down my hearing aids to tune out that old bore." She laughed and raised her sherry glass in a toast.

Sasha sipped her wine and scooted her chair closer to the woman's. "So what did you do to get sentenced to this table?" she asked in a conspiratorial tone.

36.

Phu My Port, Vietnam

L EO AND SASHA walked hand-in-hand through the crowds rushing to disembark from the cruise ships that lined the piers. Most of the vacationers were racing to catch tour buses for the two-and-a-half hour drive north to Ho Chi Minh City. But their plans didn't include any sightseeing excursions, so they strolled at a leisurely pace.

Elli and Oliver Kurck waved as they rushed by on their way to meet their tour guide.

"Have fun at the Jade Emperor Pagoda," Sasha called after them as they vanished into the crowd.

They walked in silence for a bit, then Leo said, "Are you sure you don't mind staying behind? There's really nothing to do here."

Sasha shot him a look. "Trust me, Thailand pretty much dampened my desire to go on any shore excursions."

"They don't *all* involve being chased through the streets, you know," he said, giving her a nudge.

Her easy laughter made his chest tighten.

"Says you. Anyway, I thought you wanted to visit a friend."

"I do," he agreed.

"And you promised me lunch."

"I did." He laughed to himself at the thought that she could possibly be hungry after the way she'd devoured the mussel stew and crusty bread during dinner at the captain's table last night.

"What's so funny?"

"Nothing." Leo Connelly was many things, but he wasn't stupid enough to tell a pocket-sized woman she ate like a lumberjack.

"Hmm. I would like to visit Ho Chi Minh City someday."

"So would I. But I'd like to have more than eight hours to spend in the country." Maybe, he thought, when the twins were older. They could all spend a summer in Vietnam. They'd rent a villa somewhere in the countryside between Ho Chi Minh City and Vũng Tàu and explore both cities. He could introduce Finn and Fiona to their ancestral culture, even though he himself didn't know it all that well.

They crossed through a row of empty container ship piers and walked along a narrow cobblestone path that was partially overgrown with weeds. The streets beyond the port were filled with scooters speeding by with no apparent regard for pedestrians. He kept to the path.

"This area seems very industrial," Sasha remarked.

"It is. This is a commercial zone. The cruise ships just dock here because they're too big to go up the Saigon River to Ho Chi Minh City," he explained.

He led her across a lot to a wooden ticket stand that looked like it had just received a fresh coat of red paint. She examined the map and the timetable then turned toward him. "Wait. This looks like a water taxi service. I thought you didn't want to go anywhere?"

"You're right on both counts. This is a new venture—a private hydrofoil boat that offers daily service to both Vũng Tàu to the south and Ho Chi

Minh City to the north. But we aren't buying tick-ets."

"So what are we doing?"

"You'll see." He stepped up to the window and smiled at the old woman behind the counter. He said in careful Vietnamese, *"Chào chị. Là Binh ở đây?"*

She nodded and turned away.

"Very impressive. What did you say?" Sasha asked.

"Don't be too impressed. I said—or at least I hope I said—'Hello. Is Binh here?' And that basical-ly exhausted my vocabulary."

"Binh? The man from the fishing boat?"

He nodded. "The seafarer relief organization got him a job here because he has family in a nearby village. He doesn't want to go out on the hydro-foils—I guess he's had enough boating—so he's going to help out with maintenance, office work, whatever else they need."

The wooden door set into the side of the hut opened, and a thin, tentative man stepped out into the courtyard. His eyes were fearful until he real-ized who was standing there. Then an enormous grin split his face. "Leo Nguyen!"

Sasha arched an eyebrow at the use of his fa-ther's surname, but she didn't comment.

Leo had tried to hire a translator for the day, but even the incomparable Julia was unable to find a fluent English speaker available on such short notice. So he was going to have to hope that his limited Vietnamese, Binh's equally limited English, and ample use of hand gestures would see him through. He motioned to Sasha and then to himself. "My wife. Sasha."

"Sasha," Binh repeated with a nod. He looked back at Leo with open curiosity. His expression said, 'Why are you here?'

Leo reached into the pocket of the seersucker jacket that Sasha had inexplicably packed for him and removed a piece of paper that had been folded into thirds. He offered it to Binh, who took it hesitantly. As Binh read the characters, comprehension and disbelief warred with one another on his face.

He looked up slowly and stared at Leo for a moment before speaking. "Is it real?"

"It's real. Your debt to the manning agency is gone."

Tears filled Binh's eyes. "Thank you, Leo." He turned to Sasha. "Thank you."

Leo put a hand on Binh's shoulder. "Be well, Binh."

Binh nodded, staring down at the papers in his hand.

Sasha smiled at him. "Good luck to you."

He looked up and returned her smile. Then he carefully folded the paper back into thirds and slipped it into his pocket.

Leo turned and walked back toward the pier. Sasha tripped along beside him in her ridiculous heels.

"You bought his freedom, didn't you?"

"I did. Thiha Bo's, too. That's why I was so late getting back to the ship after Ron sprang me from the clink. I had to find the scum who ran the agencies that signed them up and then keep my temper long enough to transact business—why are you laughing?"

"Sprang you from the clink? Did he get a time machine and go back to the 1950s to get you?" she teased.

"Keep it up and I won't take you to lunch. I hear this place has the best *pho* in town."

She grew serious. "*Pho*? I bet it's not as good as yours."

He wrapped his arm around her waist and pulled her close.

37.

Port of Singapore, Cruise Centre

AN'S SKIN CRAWLED and itched relentlessly. He could feel cold sweat beading on his forehead under his hat. He clenched his hands into fists at his sides and dug his fingernails in his palms.

Just hang on, he told himself. *Not long now.* He was distressed to find that he felt such an urgent need for more heroin, so soon after his visit to Vietnam. He never indulged in Singapore. The club scene was closed off, and the more readily available sources of good heroin carried a real risk of being caught. Singapore was a hard-line, law-and-order country; the accused were usually found guilty and often executed.

He stood a bit straighter as he said his goodbyes to his departing passengers. No, there was no need to tempt fate—and the death penalty. He had resisted stronger temptations than this, almost routinely. He would adhere to his rules and would wait—he *must* wait—until he returned home to The Netherlands for his upcoming leave time. A long weekend in Amsterdam would set everything right again. The very thought of it soothed him.

He smiled and exchanged pleasantries with the lovely Kurcks, Oliver and Eleanor from Finland. He managed to keep the smile pasted on his face when they were followed through the line by none other than Mr. and Mrs. Connelly. He'd managed to avoid the Americans ever since the night at sea between Laem Chabang and Phu My. Having hosted them at his personal table for dinner, he felt that he'd done more than enough to extend an olive branch on behalf of Sacred Lotus. They'd caused him an unimaginable amount of anxiety and trouble during their week-long cruise. And then Mrs. Connelly had behaved like a vagrant during dinner.

He shook their hands and wished each of them a safe flight home, genuinely pleased that he'd never have to see them again.

~ ~ ~ ~ ~ ~ ~ ~ ~ ~ ~

Sasha and Connelly said their goodbyes to the Kurcks while standing in the bustling cruise center. The Finnish couple planned to spend an additional day in Singapore, despite the dearth of chewing gum. Sasha just wanted to go home, back to her babies, and her cat and dog, and her life. Connelly apparently shared her eagerness. He'd arranged for the Singapore assistant legal attaché to meet them at the airport with statements that Mel had prepared for them to review and sign.

As Sasha and Elli exchanged hugs, email addresses, and promises to visit, Oliver helped Connelly hand off their luggage to the driver of the waiting car. A moment later, they were gliding smoothly through the city's traffic.

The driver seemed to sense that they weren't in a talkative mood. He tuned the radio to a station playing soothing instrumental music, and Sasha rested her head against the leather bench back and closed her eyes.

"Are you okay?" Connelly whispered after a while.

She nodded yes without opening her eyes. She gathered herself and then turned to him. "I'm better than okay." She grinned as she used one of his favorite lines.

"Good. We'll drop off the bags, meet the legat and get the paperwork behind us, then I want to show you something."

She arched an eyebrow at his cryptic statement, but he didn't elaborate. A moment later, the driver eased the car to a stop. The bags were whisked away, and Connelly settled up with their driver.

Inside, she found Changi Airport just as disorienting the second time as she had when they'd arrived from the U.S. a week ago. It teemed with people. Loud speaker announcements in multiple languages vied with piped-in music and hundreds of voices raised in conversation. Connelly pointed toward a lounge and they weaved their way through the throng of travelers all surging in a single direction. It reminded Sasha of swimming against a current.

After a chorus of 'pardons' and 'sorrys,' they reached the entrance to the lounge. She scanned the room and played 'Guess the Fed.' The Embassy in Singapore wasn't even *trying*. She nodded at a fresh-faced, square-jawed young man with a buzz cut and a black pinstriped suit so new she half-expected to see a sales tag dangling from the sleeve.

"That's gotta be him," she said out of the side of her mouth to Connelly. "I mean, right?"

"In the immortal words of the Magic 8-Ball, 'signs point to yes,'" he cracked as the straight-out-of-central-casting legal attaché trotted toward them.

She swallowed a giggle.

"Mr. Connelly? Ms. McCandless-Connelly?" The man stopped in front of them and stood ramrod straight, clutching a folder in his left hand.

"That's us. You must be Bartleby," Connelly said, using his G-man voice.

"Yes, sir. Michael Bartleby, Singapore ALAT, sir."

"Hi, Michael," Sasha said cheerfully, in an effort to defuse the cloud of testosterone that threatened to choke her.

"Ma'am." He nodded but didn't smile.

"How do you like working as a legat?" she asked, undaunted.

"I like it very much, ma'am." Then he softened just a touch. "Although I haven't been in the position for very long."

"You don't say, Michael." She was fairly sure she had handbags older than this kid.

"No, ma'am. I just transferred from the RSO's office."

"RSO?" she repeated blankly.

"That's a new one for me," Connelly admitted.

"Regional Security Officer," Michael helpfully supplied. "Responsible for anti-terrorism and counter-intelligence measures. Coordinates with the Singapore police on investigative matters, especially those involving Western travelers."

"Wait. I thought that's what the legal attaché does?" Sasha asked.

"Affirmative, ma'am."

She threw Connelly a baffled look.

He shrugged. "Legat is a Department of Justice position—with the Bureau. The RSO probably falls under a different authority. It's not important," he muttered then turned back to the kid. "So, Mr. Bartleby, you have some documents for us to review, correct?"

"Yes, sir. I secured a private room. Right this way."

He led them to a cramped, windowless box of a room that just managed to fit a round table and four chairs. But it had a door that closed and a light that worked, so Sasha was dutifully impressed.

Michael pulled out her chair for her and then opened his folder. He handed her a printout of a statement about her incident and a ballpoint pen. A mug shot of Derek McGraw, the man who attacked her was clipped to the front of the report. Michael handed Connelly a much thicker printout and a yellow envelope, along with another pen.

She read the statement carefully. Although she trusted Mel to get the facts right, she wanted to confirm that all the details were buttoned down. Beside her Connelly bent his head over his own statement, frowning and tapping his pen against the table as he read.

"This statement is correct, but it's incomplete," she said to the legat.

He frowned. "Incomplete how?"

"It doesn't mention the murder of the woman on the boat."

"Ma'am, my understanding is that the dead woman was not an American citizen."

"That's my understanding, too, Michael. But the reason Mr. McGraw boarded *The Water Lily* and attempted to abduct me was because I witnessed her killing. That makes it relevant. It's the motive, if you will."

Michael Bartleby had the expression of someone who'd swallowed a golf ball. He jerked his head toward Connelly looking for help. "Sir?"

Connelly glanced up from his papers. "Mina's murder—and your role as an eyewitness—is included in my report. It's covered."

She frowned. "That doesn't make any sense. I'm the one who can testify first-hand---"

Connelly leaned over and covered her hand with his. "They don't want to have anyone testifying if they can help it. This isn't federal court. Or Pennsylvania criminal court, okay? They do things differently here. And, I'm going to be completely honest with you, so don't get all pissed off—the Embassy is trying to protect you."

She bristled, but he continued before she could interrupt him. "Not because you're a woman. Or small. Or my wife. The Embassy is trying to protect you because you are an American citizen and that's their job. So let them do it."

She opened her mouth, but to her surprise no words came out. She clamped it shut so as not to look like a big, stupid fish. Then she flipped to the last page of the statement, signed and dated it, and handed it back to Michael wordlessly.

Connelly kept reading. Every couple of paragraphs, he'd mark his spot, reach into the thick yellow envelope, and pull out a labeled photograph. She craned her neck as he flipped through the photos. She caught a glimpse of a man's bare back, covered with angry red welts and then an image of a wire cage, like a large dog crate sitting on its end. She wrinkled her forehead then realized it must have been one of the cages the captain used for prisoners. Her eyes widened at the thought of Binh, crouched and cramping, trapped in that space for hours, for days. She didn't want to think about whose back that was or how the marks had gotten there.

"Is that where—"

Connelly turned the picture over and placed it image-side-down on the table. He stared into her eyes. "Please don't look at these pictures. And, yes, this is me protecting you because you're my wife. Trust me, you don't want to see this."

She nodded. "Sorry."

She stared at her hands while he finished reviewing the report. He stuffed the photographs back into the envelope, signed his name, and passed everything back to Michael. Then he stood and pushed in his chair.

"Is there anything else, Mr. Bartleby?"

The legal attaché put away the reports. "No, sir. That'll be all. And sir, ma'am, on behalf of the Director, the Bureau thanks you for your assistance in this matter. If any follow up is required or you'd like an update on the investigation, your point of contact remains ALAT Anders."

He waited for Sasha to stand up and then walked them to the door and pointed them in the direction of the customs counter before disappearing into the sea of people.

"Well, he was fun," Sasha said as he vanished into the crowd.

Connelly grinned. "He's young; he'll learn. But if I came off a little heavy handed in there, I'm sorry. I should know better."

"You did. But it's okay. I understand why."

He searched her face. "You sure?"

She stretched onto the tips of her toes and kissed him. "I'm sure. Now what did you want to show me?"

He took her hand. "You'll see."

~ ~ ~ ~ ~ ~ ~ ~ ~ ~ ~

Connelly removed his hands from her eyes. She blinked. They were standing in the middle of a lush garden, filled with hundreds of orchids. She blinked again and looked around. They were still in the terminal. And yet they were in an actual garden.

"Are these real?"

"They're real. There are over two dozen species."

The flowers were grouped by color. A koi pond and a rushing waterfall completed the indoor garden. She sat down on a low rock wall and just stared at the colors. "This is amazing," she finally said. Surreal, Vegas-like, and excessive also came to mind. But the garden *was* amazing. And breathtakingly gorgeous and dizzyingly fragrant.

"The orchid is the national flower of Singapore," he told her.

"Well aren't you just a fount of information," she cracked, smiling.

"But that's not why I brought you here." He sat down next to her and draped his arm around her shoulder.

"Oh? Then why did you?"

"Because you remind me of an orchid."

She tilted her head and waited for him to elaborate.

"People think orchids are so fragile, that they're these fussy, hothouse flowers. And a lot of them are. But some species of orchids are incredibly hardy. They have the same delicate beauty as the rest, but they're unbelievably strong. You couldn't kill them if you tried. That's the kind of orchid you are, Sasha."

She looked at him through the tears that were filling her eyes and threatening to spill over and wrinkled her nose. "That sounds more like a weed than a flower to me."

He laughed and kissed her forehead. "And that's why I'm the romantic one in this relationship."

She rested her head on his shoulder, breathed in the heady orchid perfume, and listened to the babble of the water as it coursed over the rocks.

38.

Pittsburgh, Pennsylvania

IT WAS GOOD TO be home. Leo recognized the triteness of the sentiment, but it was true all the same. Slipping back into the routines of his daily domestic life was like putting on a comfortable pair of shoes.

Judging by the way Sasha was humming as she mashed up the absolutely disgusting concoction of bananas and avocados that both Finn and Fiona appeared to love for breakfast, she felt it, too. She smiled at him from across the kitchen.

"What's on tap for you three today?" she asked. She placed a small stainless steel bowl in front of each of the twins, slid two spoons into two chubby fists, gave them each a peck on the cheek and a squeeze, and stepped back. She was already dressed for the office in a sheath dress and matching suit jacket. That meant he was on clean up duty. He should have draped the kitchen in tarps before she handed them their breakfast.

"We're going to take Mocha for a long walk through Frick Park then meet Hank and whichever Bennett kids are around at the playground."

"Sounds like fun. But no blue slide."

"Whatever, Mom."

"Connelly, I'm serious. It's too steep, and they're too little. They have years of the blue slide ahead of them. Okay?"

"Okay."

She crossed the room and gave him a long, deep kiss. "I'm glad we're home and all that ugliness is behind us."

He smiled. "Me, too. Now go earn a living so you can be back in time for dinner. I'll grill something."

"Deal." She slung her briefcase over her shoulder and waved goodbye.

He waited until he heard the door in the front of the house slam shut then looked at the twins' green- and yellow-smeared faces.

"Okay, you two. This is serious business."

They looked up at him. Fiona banged her spoon on the table.

"Nobody tell Mommy that Uncle Hank and I have been putting you on our laps and going down the blue side for, like, half your lives already. Deal?"

Finn grinned. Banana-avocado stuff oozed out of his mouth and dribbled onto his shirt.

~ ~ ~ ~ ~ ~ ~ ~ ~ ~ ~

Mocha slept, curled up in a pocket of shade under the bench where Leo and Hank sat. The dog was worn out from the trail walk through the woods. Fiona and Finn, in contrast, were tireless. They were squealing in delight as Calla and Hal, the youngest Bennetts, pushed them in the baby bucket swings.

"They're good with the babies," he remarked.

Hank regarded them with a proud parental smile. "All six of them are good kids. I think the little two get a kick out of being the big kids every once in a while. They missed the twins while you were away."

"You could have called Sasha's parents. They probably would have loved a break."

Hank laughed. "You'd think so. But their dance card was full all week. Your in-laws had them visiting cousins and friends and whatnot. They had a good time."

Leo waited a beat before changing the subject. "So I understand you bought my way out of Thai prison."

"Jail, to be precise."

"Whichever. What do I owe you?"

Hank waved a hand at the idea of repayment. "Don't worry about it."

"I am worried about it. And you should be, too. You have a half-dozen kids to put through college."

"Seriously, forget it. You can buy the pizza the next time we do combined family movie night. How bad was it?"

"The jail?"

"Yeah."

Leo considered the question. He'd spent time in police custody in the U.S. And he'd survived his training. His treatment at the hands of the Royal Thailand Police hadn't been appreciably worse. "It wasn't too bad. Not as bad as the conditions on that fishing boat."

Something in his voice must have sounded off to Hank. His boss narrowed his eyes and studied him closely. "You want to talk about it?"

He shook his head. "Nah." He didn't. He wanted to feel the sun warming his skin through his golf shirt and watch his children throw back their heads in open-mouthed laughter while Hal and Calla pushed them higher and higher.

"Well, if you change your mind—"

"I know."

They sat in silence for a moment. Then Hank said, "Looks like there's going to be a Congressional investigation into those floating armories."

"How? The feds don't have control over what happens in the middle of the freaking ocean." At least according to Sasha and all her jurisdictional, law of the sea mumbo-jumbo, they didn't.

"No, they don't," Hank agreed. "But the majority of men renting space on those armories and hiring themselves out as armed security personnel to the fleets are U.S. citizens. Mainly former military. It doesn't look good."

"All about the optics, right?"

"Something like that. McGraw and Williams are probably going to testify. If they do, they'll get immunity. How do you feel about that?"

Leo shrugged. "They're a symptom, not the cause. I mean, don't get me wrong, I'd love to run into McGraw in a dark alley." The thought of the man who'd attacked Sasha got his heart pounding a bit faster. He wondered how she'd react to the news. "Do me a favor, though?"

"What's that?"

"Don't mention the possibility to Sasha. I mean, the hearings may never come to pass, right? So why bring up an ugly memory?"

"Whatever you say." He pushed himself up from the bench. "You ready to hit that slide, old man?"

39.

ASHA RUBBED HER eyes with her fists, just as Will happened to pass by her open door.

He paused in the doorway. "Late night with the twins?"

"Yep, teething," she lied. It was easier than saying *'no, actually, my husband's tortured cries during yet another nightmare woke me up.'* And she didn't want to worry her coworkers and friends any more than she already had. Ever since she'd told Will and Naya about the events that transpired on the least relaxing luxury cruise ever, they'd been tiptoeing around her as if she were made of china.

"Brew some chamomile tea, dip those little baby washcloths in it, and then freeze them. Next time they get fussy, give them the frozen washcloths to gnaw on. Works like a charm." He smiled, no doubt at a memory of his now-adult sons' teething days.

"Thanks for the tip. I'll have to remember that."

"Any time." He strolled away looking pleased with himself for being so helpful.

She turned her attention back to the motion *in limine* she was drafting, but part of her mind stayed on the subject of Connelly and his dreams. They didn't wake him, he never mentioned them in the morning, but ever since they'd returned from their cruise, he'd been having terrible dreams. At least they *sounded* terrible. She nibbled on the end of her pen and wondered exactly what he'd seen on the fishing boat.

She worked steadily through lunch and only re-alized she'd missed the meal when her stomach growled loudly. She saved her file, capped her pen, and was halfway out the door to grab a wrap from Jake's downstairs, when her office line rang. She hesitated in the doorway, trying to decide whether to ignore it or go back and answer it. Caroline picked up the line, mooting the entire issue.

"Sasha McCandless-Connelly's office. How may I help you?" she chirped.

Sasha lingered near Caroline's workstation, waiting to hear who was calling. Caroline placed the caller on hold and looked up. "It's a Mel Anders calling from the United States Embassy in Bangkok."

"I'll take it. Just give me a minute to get back to my desk."

"Of course," Caroline said to her back. "Do you want me to run down and get you a sandwich?"

Sasha smiled. Will's secretary didn't miss a thing. "Thanks. That would be awesome," she called over her shoulder before pulling her door shut and picking up the call.

"Hey, Mel," she said as she adjusted her hands-free headset on her head and sank into her chair. "How are things in Thailand?"

"Hey, yourself," Mel answered. "Life in paradise continues to be paradisiacal. And Pittsburgh?"

Sasha glanced at her window. The sky was dark gray, heavy with fat rain clouds. The July day promised thunderstorms, which would be a welcome respite from temperatures in the high nineties with ninety percent humidity. "Also a paradise," she deadpanned. "So, are you just calling to talk about the weather or ...?"

"I have an update for you. Actually, two."

Sasha tamped down her surprise that Mel was calling her, rather than Connelly. "Lay it on me."

"Well, the dynamic duo of Austin Williams and Derek McGraw have been charged with attempted kidnapping, technically an offense against liberty."

"What about murder?" Sasha sputtered.

"Simmer down. The murder charge is tricky—"

"Jurisdictionally?" The murder of a Malaysian woman by American citizens on a Cambodian-flagged boat in Thailand's territorial waters was something out of a Conflicts of Law final exam, she'd grant that. But there were arguments that could be crafted.

"Not just jurisdictionally. Politically, there's just not a lot of will to prosecute. A cross-border team finally found Mina's family in a small village in Northern Malaysia, but they're a couple of teens themselves—the parents are deceased, the girls are just scraping by. They don't have the stomach, or frankly the money, to advocate for their dead sister."

"I'll cover whatever costs are involved," Sasha insisted.

"Just hear me out. These defense contractors or whatever they call themselves aren't stupid. They found good attorneys, who are looking for a deal to get rid of the kidnapping case. And the authorities would love for that to happen—nobody wants the publicity that would come from a case involving the attempted kidnapping of an American professional on an upscale holiday in Southeast Asia—not the tourism ministry, not Sacred Lotus, and certainly not the Embassy."

Lawyers, Sasha thought with disgust, conveniently forgetting for the moment that she was one.

"What kind of deal are we talking about? Can they at least shut down that blasted armory? Is the IMO involved?" she asked.

Mel snorted. "No, the IMO's official position on mercenaries on shipping vessels, or as it so delicately puts it 'privately contracted armed security personnel,' is that it takes no official position—it leaves that issue, and by extension, the floating armories that supply the firepower—to the flag states and the coastal states that are affected."

"Ugh. International diplomats sound just about entirely spineless."

"McGraw and Williams are providing information about some of Thale's shady business dealings, which take place firmly within Thailand's borders—no law of the sea to worry about, no cross-jurisdictional coordination required, no stonewalling from the Cambodian shipping registry. The Thai authorities are pretty sure they can nail Thale to the wall."

One of her Nana Alexandrov's favorite sayings popped into her head: *A half a loaf is better than a poke in the eye.* It was a misquote, two aphorisms mashed together, but it always made her smile.

"That's something."

"Oh, it's *a lot.* Thale's involved in heroin trafficking—as in, it's a big player. Our local DEA agents are raring to get a warrant to search the fishing fleet, and, from what I understand, the people in the Royal Thailand Police Narcotics Suppression Bureau are pretty fired up, too. I know it's sort of attenuated, but if Williams and McGraw give up the goods on Thale's drug smuggling activities in exchange for clemency, it's going to help a lot of girls like Mina—and the men who were on that ship."

"I guess."

"But, here's the thing—that means they won't do any time. Are you okay with that? I mean, they were planning to kill you."

She knew, intellectually, that they hadn't been planning to throw her a party, but hearing Mel say the words—those men would have shot her and left her for the sharks—chilled her.

"This heroin ring is real? And shutting it down will be for the greater good—you're sure, right?"

"Positive."

"Then do what you need to do." It suddenly became clear why Mel had called her and not Connelly. He was going to go ballistic when he heard about this.

Mel let out a relieved sigh. "I'm glad you understand. Trust me, though, this is going to be big. Really big."

"I'm glad."

Caroline eased the door open and waved a white paper bag at Sasha. She motioned for her to come in. Caroline placed the takeout order on Sasha's desk. 'Thanks,' she mouthed. She'd figure out what she owed Caroline after the call.

She peeked inside the bag---tomato, mozzarella, and pesto on Jake's homemade flatbread. Reluctantly, she put the food aside and returned her focus to the call.

"There's one more thing," Mel was saying.

"What's that?"

"This is going to sound crazy, but in retrospect it makes sense. Bar Pavot came up in the interviews with McGraw and Williams."

Bar Pavot? The cute, little French-inspired bistro. The one they'd been chased from by a gunman. In light of the circumstances, it sounded plausible.

"What's the connection? Oh, wait—was the creepy American who you caught staring at us one of those two?"

"Nope. I've spent enough time staring their ugly mugs to be sure that neither Derek nor Austin was at the bar. But the joint is partially owned by a Thale entity. *And* they apparently were selling heroin out of the back room. *Pavot*, poppy—get it?"

"Classy."

"Right? I was invited to tag along with The Royal Police when they raided Bar Pavot this morning and you'll never believe what they found."

She couldn't even hazard a guess. It could be anything. "Tell me."

"In a safe in the drug room, there was a wooden box containing heroin cigarettes. That monstrous Thai who chased us was manning the door. When he saw my face he started talking fast. That box and its contents allegedly belong to one Jan van Metier, Captain with The Sacred Lotus Cruise Line."

Sasha's heart skipped a beat and then, as if to make up for it, thumped crazily, in double time. Captain van Metier, a heroin user? Who just *happened* to frequent Bar Pavot? Her hands shook as she pulled up the file of pictures from the cruise and started to scroll through the thumbnails until she found the one of her and Connelly suffering through dinner at the Captain's Table. She stared at the captain's cold, regal face for a moment.

"The American who was staring at us at the bar, you said he was older?"

"Right. He seemed like a completely respectable guy, except for the part where he was leering at us. Did you hear me? Van Metier is a drug user *and* he's connected, at least as a customer, to Thale."

"I heard you. I'm going to email you a picture." She dragged the jpeg into her email program and typed in Mel's email address. She tapped 'send.' "Okay, it went. Tell me when you get it."

"Got it."

Sasha waited a beat, then she heard Mel exhale, a loud *whooshing* noise.

"That's him, the guy from the bar."

"That's Captain Jan van Metier."

They sat in mutual silence for a moment. Then Mel said, "He transferred to another ship. He's not captaining *The Water Lily* anymore. I'm sure that's not a coincidence. I doubt he'll be sailing into any jurisdiction where I can grab him easily for questioning."

Sasha coughed. "Leave van Metier to me. And Mel?"

"Yeah."

"Do me a favor and don't mention this to Ron just yet. I don't want it getting back to Connelly until I have a plan."

~ ~ ~ ~ ~ ~ ~ ~ ~ ~ ~

By dinnertime, she had a plan. Or at least, she thought she did. She looked up from the stack of regulations she'd spent the afternoon reading and pawed around on her desk until she found the telephone headset under a legal notebook. She put it on and called Connelly.

"You're walking out the door, right?" he answered in a hopeful tone.

She winced. She could hear two cranky babies in the background. It was the nightly witching hour—they seemed to get grumpy in that last bit of time just before she got home to relieve Connelly and right when he was at his busiest trying to get dinner on the table. "Soon. I have to make one more phone call."

"Is it important?"

"It really is."

"And it's really just *one* call?"

"One call. I swear," she promised.

"Be careful walking home."

"Am I ever not careful?"

"I know that distracted, wrapped up in a case voice, Sasha. You're a thousand miles away. Just pay attention during the walk."

"Yes, Mom."

He ignored her snark. "And stop in at that pet store on Ellsworth and get Java some food, okay? Make sure it's the grain-free stuff with the duck and vegetables, no fish. Ask someone if you're not sure."

"Wait—the all-natural, organic pet store?"

"That's the one."

She pursed her lips. "Did the vet say to change her food?"

"No. But that whitefish stuff we've been feeding her is imported by a company with ties to Thale."

"Thale? The Thale Group for Thailand."

"Right. They supply fish to most of the big American pet food companies, and the company that makes Java's food can't confirm that the fish isn't sourced from boats using sea slaves. There could be men like Binh living—and dying—in squalor so we can buy cat food for a quarter a can."

"Did you call up the cat food company and ask them?"

"Actually, I did. Why?"

"Just curious. We probably should be more careful about where we spend our money. Will was just telling me about the big chocolate companies using cocoa beans harvested by child slaves in West Africa."

"That's disgusting."

They sat in heavy silence for a moment.

Then she said, "I'll be home as soon as I can."

"Sounds good. I love you."

"Love you more." She ended the call and stared at the phone in her hand and wondered, *Just how deep did his scars from that fishing boat run?* After a long moment, she shook herself back to the present and the task at hand.

She did a quick internet search for Professor Alfredson's phone number then placed the call. Her former admiralty law professor answered his phone on the second ring. His voice was softer than she'd remembered, but still strong.

She took a breath and plowed into her spiel. "Professor Alfredson, my name is Sasha McCandless-Connelly. You probably don't remember me but I took your Law of the Sea course in—"

"In 2003, I believe it was. You were just Sasha McCandless then. But yes, I remember you, counselor. The tiny spitfire with the left hook that scared all the boxers." He chuckled, and she could picture him, his hands folded over his belly as he shook with laughter.

"Guilty as charged, professor."

"I read the papers, you know, online. I understand you're making quite a name for yourself with your own law firm and everything."

He read about her in the newspapers because she seemed to attract danger, not because of her legal acumen, but she let the statement pass unchallenged. "I was wondering if you could help me out with a case. Just a quick phone consultation," she promised.

"I'd be glad to let you pick my brain, young lady. Since my retirement, I've had a steady diet of crosswords, Sudoku, and historical nonfiction, with the occasional thriller novel thrown in for good measure. A legal issue would be a refreshing change of pace."

She believed him. The enthusiasm in his voice was unmistakable.

"Great, thank you. Don't get too excited. It's not the most esoteric question."

"Please, ask away."

She scanned her notes for a moment before she began to speak; then she turned them face down so as not to be distracted by them. "Okay, the issue arises under the federal Cruise Vessel Security and Safety Act of 2010. Are you familiar with it?"

"Ah, yes, the CVSSA, signed into law in 2012. I know it well. I gave testimony to Congress when it was being considered."

Perfect.

"Here's the fact pattern. An American citizen is aboard a Bahamian-flagged ship that embarks and disembarks in Singapore. So far, the act doesn't apply, correct?"

"Correct."

"But the cruise line is owned by a Delaware corporation."

"The Act may apply." He stated his opinion instantly and with professorial conviction.

She pumped her fist. "It only applies if the criminal act occurs in U.S. waters or if the crime involves a U.S. national as either the victim or the perpetrator and the crime occurs in waters where no nation has jurisdiction. Right?"

"Correct again, Ms. McCandless. Just like the old days."

She felt a blush creep up her cheeks and shook her head at herself. Old crushes die hard.

"Here's the million-dollar question, professor: what if neither the victim nor the perpetrator is *on* the U.S.-owned cruise ship?"

He was silent for a solid minute. "I'm afraid I can't conceive of a fact pattern that would fit."

"Say a passenger on the cruise ship, which is, let's say hypothetically, at sea in the Gulf of Thailand in an area of disputed jurisdiction."

"That describes much of the Gulf of Thailand," he said with a laugh.

"The bit that has caused so many territorial flare-ups that no one is eager to claim it."

"Gray waters."

"Exactly. So, our ship is in gray waters and a passenger witnesses a U.S. national committing a crime on another boat out at sea."

"The cruise passenger witnesses the crime, you say?"

"Yes, and she's a U.S. citizen, but that doesn't matter does it?"

He *hmmed* thoughtfully then said, "No, it doesn't. And the victim's nationality?"

"Not a citizen of the United States."

"But the perpetrator is?"

"Correct. And just to make it murkier, the boat on which the crime occurred is neither U.S.-flagged nor U.S.-owned. In fact, it's not even a cruise ship."

He cackled. "This is a cracking good fact pattern, Sasha. I trust the crime itself is one of the crimes enumerated in the Act?"

"It's a murder."

"Definitely covered. So lay out your argument."

Suddenly, she was twenty-five years old again. She exhaled and spoke slowly. "Under the clear language of the CVSSA, there's been an incident involving homicide on a cruise line owned by a United States corporation; the incident has occurred on the high seas; and the perpetrator is a United States national. Accordingly, the owner of the cruise line had a duty to report the crime to the nearest legal attaché by telephone as soon as possible and to submit a written report through the Internet portal set up under the Act."

"And the incident involving homicide that occurred on the cruise ship was that a passenger witnessed the crime, do I have that right?"

"Yes." She held her breath. This part was the weakest link in a not overly strong argument.

"It's certainly not something I think Congress contemplated. But I think, yes, it falls within the purview of the Act."

Sasha grinned in triumph. "I can't thank you enough, Professor Alfredson," she gushed.

"It was my pure pleasure, Sasha. Call anytime. Now, I hate to rush you off the phone, but I'm afraid my pinochle club is waiting impatiently for me." He ended the call.

Sasha tossed the headset on her mess of a desk and scribbled a note to leave on Naya's desk on her way out. Then she grabbed her purse and turned off the lights.

40.

NAYA WAS PERCHED on the edge of Sasha's desk when Sasha walked into the office at seven-thirty in the morning.

"About time you got here," Naya cracked.

Sasha took a sip of her coffee and surveyed her desk. "You moved my piles."

"What piles? That was just a whole mess of papers sliding into each other. I put them into neat stacks for you, Mac."

Sasha tried to ignore the worry that was worming its way into her brain. "How am I going to find anything?" she wondered.

Naya flapped her hand. "Never mind that. I have a surprise for you."

"What's that?"

"I found Captain van Metier."

Sasha rested her mug on the coaster that Naya had evidently unearthed during her cleaning spree. "Already? I mean, I knew you were good—"

"Oh, yeah. I'm *that* good." She picked up a printout from the desk and handed it to Sasha. "He's still with Sacred Lotus. He's now the captain of *The Viola*, which cruises from Baltimore to Quebec City."

"He's *here?*"

"No, he's not here. He's ... well, give me that back." She took the paper from Sasha's hand. "He's currently somewhere between Boston and Baltimore on his way back from Canada."

"Right, but he's here in the United States."

"Sure, okay." Naya eyed her cautiously.

"Let me see that timetable again, please?" Naya handed it over, and Sasha studied it for a moment. "What's on your schedule for tomorrow?"

Naya unlocked her iPhone screen and pulled up her calendar. "Women's Bar Association meeting. And I'm supposed to get my teeth cleaned. Why?"

"Can you call up your dentist and reschedule? I need someone to serve Captain van Metier with a deposition notice."

"I'm happy to road trip to Baltimore, Mac. But there's one small flaw with your plan. You don't have a pending case against the captain or Sacred Lotus."

"True. But the Pennsylvania Rules of Civil Procedure allow for pre-complaint discovery."

Naya nodded. "Sure. But this is about what happened on the cruise, right? The attack?"

"It's actually about the girl."

"The Malaysian teenager who was killed on the Cambodian-flagged, Thai-owned fishing boat?"

"That's the one."

"And you're going to sue the cruise line in the Commonwealth of Pennsylvania?"

"Yes. Well, maybe. I might just sue van Metier personally," Sasha nodded.

"Do me a favor. Keep my name off these papers."

Sasha shot Naya a look. "That stings. You don't think I can pull this off? But, that's fine I'll draft it and sign it, if you'll serve it."

"You've got yourself a deal."

"Excellent. Please get your butt off my desk so I can get started. And don't forget to call your dentist's office."

Naya started toward the door but stopped and gave Sasha a serious look. "I'm saying this as a friend. This is quite possibly the most farfetched thing you've ever proposed. Do yourself a favor and run it by Will first."

~ ~ ~ ~ ~ ~ ~ ~ ~ ~

Will, not surprisingly, took some convincing. But he eventually agreed that if Sasha commenced an action against Jan van Metier by filing a praecipe for a writ, then the Commonwealth of Pennsylvania's liberal pre-complaint discovery rules would permit her to begin to gather sufficient information to enable her to file a complaint.

"But, you realize if you do file a complaint, Sacred Lotus will almost certainly seek to remove the case to federal court. And, frankly, a removal motion would be a winner, don't you agree?" Will cautioned.

"Probably. But I don't even intend to get that far. Once Jan van Metier appears for his deposition, it'll be game, set, match," she explained with a confidence she didn't quite feel.

"What makes you think he'll roll over?"

"He won't tell Sacred Lotus that I've served him. You don't know the guy, Will. He's very concerned about appearances—and arrogant as all get out. He reminds me of Cinco."

Will groaned at the mention of their former boss—the one-time managing partner of Prescott & Talbott. Cinco was dangerously overconfident. Sasha thought the same could fairly be said about a man who was comfortable using heroin and piloting a one-hundred-thousand-ton boat loaded with people. But she didn't want to get into those details with Will.

She went on. "He'll come down here from Baltimore during his next shore leave, expecting to be able to talk his way out of this. But there's no way out. He didn't do the requisite paperwork. He's toast."

"It's like nailing Al Capone for tax evasion, Sasha. You're getting him on a technicality."

"I don't care how I get him, Will. I just want him off the seas. And the feds have different priorities."

Will looked at her closely. "What's Leo think about this?"

Sasha had a convenient coughing fit, and by the time Caroline brought her a glass of water, Will had forgotten there was a question pending—or had the decency to pretend he'd forgotten.

She did plan to talk to Connelly. She truly did. She just needed to find a time when he wasn't obsessing about cat food and they weren't both juggling babies.

41.

J AN WALKED UP the ramp to the nearly empty terminal waiting area. The last of *The Viola's* disembarking passengers had cleared out, and he was about to begin a week-long leave. His first in Baltimore.

His understanding was that the heroin trade was brisk here—the city apparently served as the starting point of the East Coast's bustling drug corridor. He had no doubt that he'd find a new side job in quick order. But the rules of shuttling were etched in stone: one never stole from one's employer. Although the temptation was always there, to act on the urge would be suicidal. That was why he'd sought out places like Bar Pavot.

He felt a wave of worry, though, at the prospect of satisfying his needs in a new community. He'd have to find a club that would both afford him the quality of heroin he'd grown accustomed to in Southeast Asia and would protect his privacy. Until then, he'd ration the cigarettes he'd brought with him from Amsterdam. He patted his side pocket, where they were safely tucked away and scanned the terminal in all directions to confirm that no drug-sniffing dogs were on patrol.

When he turned his head back, he stopped in his tracks. He'd nearly plowed directly into a trim, African-American woman. She seemed to have materialized out of nowhere and was standing less than two feet from him.

"I'm terribly sorry, ma'am."

"No worries. Hey, aren't you Captain Jan van Metier?" she said in a voice that hinted at awe—or at least admiration.

He examined her more closely. He had continued his habit of matching passenger faces to manifests, but *The Viola* was a significantly larger ship than was *The Water Lily*, and he had not yet met each member of his crew personally. He frowned slightly and bowed from his waist. "I am, indeed. But I'm afraid I can't place you. Have we met?"

The woman smiled broadly and extended her right hand as if she were offering a handshake. He extended his own, then he noticed that she was holding an envelope.

"We haven't, but this is for you," she said pleasantly, still smiling.

He took the envelope reflexively. Before he could thank her, the courier, whoever she was, had walked off, into the heart of the terminal.

He looked down at the envelope. It bore no writing. He slit open the seal with the edge of his thumbnail and removed a document. He lowered himself into a molded plastic seat and skimmed the contents. It was a legal document captioned *Sasha McCandless-Connelly v. Jan van Metier.*

What the deuce?

It seemed as though the blasted Connelly woman intended to sue him—him, personally—in court in Pennsylvania, of all places. The paper demanded that he appear in person in Pittsburgh to answer questions regarding his maintenance while Captain of *The Water Lily* of a log book required pursuant to Title 46 of The United States Code, also known as the Cruise Vessel Security and Safety Act, as well as questions regarding his "mental fitness" to command his ship. She claimed to need this information in order to file a complaint. His spine stiffened.

The woman's concerns about the log book were born of ignorance and easily explained away—she'd been attacked while the ship was docked in Laem Chabang, and he'd reported the attack to the proper authorities. He wasn't required to log such an incident under the Act. As for the issue of whether he was mentally fit to do his job, her impertinence was an outrage.

He pocketed the papers and stormed out of the terminal. This would not stand.

~ ~ ~ ~ ~ ~ ~ ~ ~ ~ ~

"Got him." Even through the cell phone connection, Naya's voice rang with triumph.

Sasha stood and paced around her office. She had to burn some energy. "Where are you?"

"I'm sitting in my car, parked illegally, by the way, across from the cruise terminal. I waited until his passengers had unloaded—"

"Disembarked, actually."

"It's rude to interrupt, *actually*."

"Sorry. Go ahead."

"So after the passengers had *disembarked*, I hung out near the gangway, or ramp, or whatever you call it until the crew started to straggle out. When I spotted the captain, I sort of just stalked him through the terminal until he was distracted, then boom! I sidled up to him pretty as you please and served his ass."

Sasha had to smile at the glee in Naya's voice. That woman loved serving legal process more than any human being she'd ever met. She was probably wasting her talents as a lawyer. She'd be a reality television sensation if she started a show called Naya Andrews, Process Server.

"I hope you didn't hang around to see his reaction?"

"Girl, no. I skedaddled. But I jumped in my car and figured I'd see if he came out soon. And he sure did. His face was like thunder. He's hopping mad. But you know, you just may be right. He might be crazy enough to show up unrepresented." She cackled at the thought.

"Oh, I'm right, all right. Good work. Now get back here and I'll buy you a celebratory beer."

"Margarita."

"Done."

Sasha disconnected the call and returned to her desk. If the captain had, in fact, taken the bait, she had some work to do.

42.

I T WAS LATE when Sasha returned home from work. So late that not only were the kids both sleeping, but so were the dog, the cat, and the husband. She surveyed her living room. It looked like the aftermath of a raging party, with people passed out on every horizontal surface.

She stood inside the doorway and removed her stilettos. Then she tiptoed across the room and picked Finn up from the blanket on the floor. She crept up the stairs and put him to bed. She waited for a moment, listening and watching to make sure he stayed asleep, then repeated the process with Fiona.

By the time she returned to the living room, Connelly was half-awake and blinking as his eyes adjusted to the light.

"You're home."

"You're observant."

He grinned. "Long day?"

She nodded and crossed the room to perch on the arm of the chair in which he was sitting. He ran his hand along her arm.

"Sorry if I woke you."

"I wasn't sleeping."

She pulled a face at the obvious fib. "Right."

"I was resting. Did you eat?"

"We ordered in."

"We? Are you working on something big?"

"Sort of. Naya and Will offered to help me out. If you're awake, why don't you come into the kitchen and I'll tell you all about it while I get a glass of water?"

He trailed her to the kitchen and leaned against the counter while she poured them each a glass of water.

"So I've been meaning to tell you about this, but things have been hectic ever since we got back from the cruise," she began, hoping she didn't sound as defensive to his ears as she did to her own.

"Mmm-hmm." He put down his glass and folded his arms across his chest.

Okay, so that answered that. She did sound defensive.

"Anyway, I got a call from Mel a few days ago—"

"Mel Anders?"

"The one and only." She sipped her water. "She wanted to let me know that Williams and McGraw are going to make a deal with the Thai authorities. Basically, they're giving up Thale, which apparently is a good-sized heroin trafficker, in exchange for immunity."

"Son of a ..."

"Hang on. I told Mel I was okay with it."

He shook his head. "A few days ago, Hank told me that McGraw and Williams are going to testify at Congressional hearings into the floating armory situation in exchange for immunity. So, they won't be charged in Thailand or here." His voice dripped with disgust. "I know you wanted to see justice for Mina. I'm sorry, babe."

"They obviously have competent defense attorneys. And Mel said that the Malaysian authorities don't plan to investigate Mina's murder either, which was pretty disheartening, I'll admit. But here comes the awesome part." She grinned at him.

"Mel also mentioned that Captain van Metier is a heroin user."

"What?" He furrowed his forehead and tilted his head.

"I know, right? He was buying from Thale. *He's* the guy who was staring at me and Mel in that bistro. He was there doing drugs in a backroom. I'm sure he freaked out when he saw me there, too."

"He's the one who told Thale that you witnessed the murder," Connelly said slowly.

"And he *let* McGraw and Williams board the ship. *And* I totally didn't put this together at the time, but he came to our room to lend me a cell phone when I was trying to reach you. By which I mean he, personally, was the last person to enter the suite before McGraw and Williams went in guns blazing—and Connelly, I watched from Elli's deck. Our door wasn't locked. He *helped* them."

"Are you sure?" His face clouded with anger.

"I'm sure enough that I filed a praecipe for a writ and served pre-complaint discovery on him. He's coming to the office tomorrow to answer questions. And he's so full of himself that he hasn't told Sacred Lotus *or* retained counsel to represent him."

"Wait? He's coming here? To Pittsburgh? From Singapore?"

"He transferred to a different ship. I'm sure Southeast Asia was getting a little too hot for comfort with the narcotics bureau investigating his supplier. He's piloting a Baltimore to Quebec City route. He's stationed out of Baltimore. Naya drove down there and served him earlier today."

Connelly gaped at her for a moment. "Well, I guess this answers the question of what you do all day long."

She laughed. "Here's where you come in." She took a deep breath. "Do you and Hank have the authority under whatever unofficial department you don't work for to arrest him or detain him or whatever it is you do to bad guys, unofficially?"

He scrunched up his face. "On what charges, exactly?"

She thought. "Well, I'm going to get him to say he didn't log the incident as he was required to do under the CVSSA when I reported Mina's murder. That's a civil violation, not very sexy, I know. But if you and Hank could get one of the hired guns—McGraw or Williams or both—to corroborate that van Metier *told* Thale that I witnessed the murder *and* gave them access to me on the ship, then I can establish that he *willfully* violated the regulation. He deliberately didn't log my report of Mina's murder in an effort to protect his drug dealer. A willful violation is punishable by a fine of a quarter million dollars, up to a year in prison, or both."

He grabbed her by the shoulders and planted a quick, hard kiss on her lips. "You're a freaking genius."

She smiled. She was pretty jazzed, too, but it was important to temper his expectations. "Well, to be completely honest this entire argument is premised on a fairly attenuated reading of the statute."

He deflated. "Oh."

"But," she continued brightly, "it really doesn't matter."

"Why not?"

"Because I'm betting he's going to have heroin on his person when he shows up tomorrow. You can definitely charge him for that, right?"

Connelly swatted her butt playfully. "You bet your sweet ass we can!"

"Language, Connelly."

That earned her another swat.

"Stop that. It's time for bed. Tomorrow's a big day." She drained her glass and placed it in the sink.

43.

J AN CHECKED HIS uniform in the hotel's full-length mirror to ensure that it was sharply pressed and wrinkle-free. The jacket hung perfectly from his shoulders. His trousers were creased precisely. And his shoes were polished to a high shine. He nodded approvingly at his reflection. The impression he made would matter.

After all, today was a big day. He needed to remain calm, educate Sasha McCandless-Connelly as to the fallacy of her thinking, and deflect her ridiculous criticism of his competence—mental or otherwise. These tasks would be facile in the extreme as long as he maintained his equanimity. He would be dispassionate, patient, and unflappable in the face of her no-doubt misguided questioning.

He patted his pocket reflexively. He had five cigarettes left. A smoke would help him relax. He consulted his watch. He had plenty of time. He unbuttoned his jacket and carefully hung it on a padded hanger. Then he removed his slim cigarette case and selected a cigarette. He lit the end and reclined on the couch under the plate-glass window. He inhaled deeply and closed his eyes. It was time to get loose.

~ ~ ~ ~ ~ ~ ~ ~ ~ ~

Sasha arrived at the office while the sun was still just a pink-orange ribbon in the sky and shut herself in the conference room. She reviewed her deposition outline twice, went downstairs to Jake's and ordered a large coffee, then reviewed the outline twice more.

Preparation was her watchword, always—but *especially* when her adversary was self-important and arrogant. A man like Jan van Metier had an inflated sense of his own cleverness. He'd been nearly insufferable on his own ship at his dinner table, when he'd insisted on schooling her on the history of the Royal Netherlands Navy. She could only imagine the performance he'd turn in on her turf—her office, her area of expertise. He'd hang himself.

Her job was simply to give him the rope, bit by bit, slowly, so slowly that he wouldn't realize he'd created a noose until it was strung around his neck.

She shivered at her own morbid metaphor. She typically wasn't so ... pitched ... before battle. But she'd had a visceral reaction to the man from the very beginning. Knowing that he tried to aid and abet her would-be killers had only made her more determined to knock him down a peg—or seven.

She checked her watch. She had time for one more mug of coffee and another read through of the outline before the court reporter arrived. She exhaled slowly and rolled her shoulders like a boxer before a match. It was time to get loose.

~ ~ ~ ~ ~ ~ ~ ~ ~ ~

Hank, who was not a morning person under the best of circumstances, was grousing nearly non-stop.

Leo glanced up from the article he was reading. "What's wrong with you today?"

Hank gestured around Sasha's office, where they'd been holed up for the better part of an hour. "This is a dumb plan, Leo. We're going to sit around in the office watching a live video feed of a deposition and do what again?"

Leo gave Hank a look. "I know you were listening when Sasha ran through this. She's having the court reporter videotape the deposition, which is apparently fairly standard for pretrial discovery. We're going to watch the feed in here on her monitor. When van Metier says something that implicates him in a regulatory violation or amounts to an admission that he's a drug user, we're supposed to go next door to the conference room and take him into custody."

"Regulatory violation," Hank muttered under his breath. "We're just supposed to magically know he's got heroin on him. Harebrained scheme."

Leo narrowed his eyes. "What did you have for breakfast?"

Hank started to grumble a response, but Leo cut him off. "Cole's got you on the low-fat, low-carb egg white diet again, doesn't he?" He picked up Sasha's desk phone and pressed the number for reception.

"Hi, Caroline. You know that candy bar commercial with the hungry, excuse me, *hangry* grouch?"

"Yes?"

"I have one of those in here. It's getting ugly. Could you have Jake send us up a couple of the greasiest breakfast sandwiches they can put together?" He took another look at his boss. "And a couple donuts, just to be safe."

Caroline's silvery laughter tinkled in his ear. "I'll make sure to feed the bear."

"Thanks. You might want to put a rush on it. I'm unarmed in here."

He ended the call.

"I might be cranky," Hank admitted. "But it's not egg whites this time. It's oatmeal. Unsweetened, unflavored oatmeal." He shuddered at the memory. "You better not have been telling the truth just now—are you really not carrying?"

"Why? You going to shoot me if Jake forgets the bacon?"

"Leo," Hank warned.

"I have my Glock. I just didn't think I should announce it to the world."

"Or Sasha's receptionist," Hank shot back.

"That, too."

Hank managed a half-laugh.

Good, Leo thought. They should treat this just like any other stakeout. It was important to stay loose.

44.

AT PRECISELY TEN O'CLOCK, after positioning the camera so that the deponent was centered in the frame, the stenographer/videographer pressed the buttons to begin recording. Through some magic that Sasha couldn't fully understand but always appreciated, the final video and the typed transcript would sync perfectly. Then the court reporter swore in van Metier and gave Sasha the nod to start.

She glanced down at her outline, then closed the folder, and pushed it to the side. She folded her hands in front of her on the table and smiled at Captain van Metier. He did not smile back at her.

"Good morning, Captain. As you know, my name is Sasha McCandless-Connelly. This deposition arises in a somewhat unusual procedural posture, so let me state for the record that this is a pre-complaint deposition taken to elicit information sufficient to allow me to state my claim in the matter of *McCandless-Connelly v. van Metier*. This deposition is limited to the two areas of inquiry set forth in the Notice of Deposition served in this matter."

She pushed a copy of the notice across the table. "Do you recognize this document?"

"Yes. These are the legal papers that were handed to me when I returned from a six-day international cruise between Quebec City, Canada, and Baltimore, Maryland."

Sasha managed not to smile. He was a dream deponent. The answer to her question—the full and complete answer, which any attorney worth his or her salt would have prepared a client to give—was simply 'yes.'

"Let the record reflect this is a true and correct copy of the Notice of Deposition of Jan van Metier, which has been pre-marked as Exhibit A." She passed a copy to the court reporter then continued.

"Now that we've got that out of the way, could you please state and spell your full name for the record?"

"I am Captain Jan van Metier, J-A-N V-A-N M-E-T-I-E-R, Captain of the Sacred Lotus ship *The Viola*, previously Captain of *The Water Lily*, and retired from the Royal Netherlands Navy with the rank of Warrant Officer 1."

The court reporter shot Sasha a 'is this guy serious' look? Sasha didn't react.

"Captain van Metier, are you represented by counsel?"

"Do you see another attorney here?"

Ordinarily, Sasha would have reined him in right away, but she was perfectly content to let him get on a roll. So she simply said, "I'll take that as a no."

"You take it any way you like."

She ignored the commentary. "Have you ever been deposed before?"

"No, I have not, and if you would kindly cut to the chase and ask me your questions, I could dispose of them in short order and we could both get on with our days."

She decided it was time to rile him up a bit more. "I'm afraid I can't do that. It's important that I explain how this process works so you're not confused. I know the legal system can be hard to understand." She smiled sweetly.

His ruddy face reddened to a shade deeper. "I'm not confused in the least."

"All the same, I need to make sure there's no misunderstanding. In this deposition, I'll ask the questions and you'll answer them. Do you understand?"

"Yes, I understand."

"Do you understand that you've taken an oath to answer my questions fully and honestly to the best of your ability?"

"Yes."

"Good. Is there any reason, such as being under unusual stress, suffering from a physical or mental condition, or being under the influence of any substances, that would limit your ability to give truthful and complete answers to my questions today?" Her mind wandered to the last deponent who had answered that question in the affirmative—Laura Yim, who was distracted by what she perceived as a threat and who was later killed by a dirty FBI agent. She forced her focus back to the present. This was the money question; she needed to be attentive.

"Of course not," he bristled. He patted his right jacket pocket.

"Are you certain?"

"Am I certain? Madam, what are you suggesting?"

"Please remember, Captain, I ask the questions,
you answer the questions. Do you understand?"

"Yes, I understand."

"Good. Please state your current home address
for the record."

~ ~ ~ ~ ~ ~ ~ ~ ~ ~

Hank groaned. Leo knew the feeling. He
propped his feet up on Sasha's desk and tried not
to scream as she walked Captain van Metier
through his educational background and military
service in excruciating detail. Sasha's deposition
had been underway for at least thirty minutes, and
she still hadn't asked him any real questions.

On the live feed, Sasha paused, breaking the
monotonous rhythm of her monotonous questioning. He leaned forward, hopeful. Hank sat up
straighter. Maybe this was it.

"Let's move on to your employment history,"
Sasha said. "We'll start with your first position after you retired from the Navy. Who was your employer then?"

Back in her office, Leo felt something like des-
pair settle over him.

~ ~ ~ ~ ~ ~ ~ ~ ~ ~

Sasha scanned her notes to confirm she'd covered all the preliminaries then said, "Let's get to the substance, shall we?"

"Yes, let's," the captain agreed through clenched teeth.

"Are you familiar with the Cruise Vessel Safety and Security Act of 2010?"

"Yes, of course. It requires a cruise ship operator, such as Sacred Lotus, which is owned by an American company, to report and document certain crimes that occur at sea under certain circumstances, *none* of which exist in this case, I assure you."

"Let's explore that. When you say 'this case' are you referring to the incident in which Derek McGraw and Austin Williams boarded *The Water Lily* in an attempt to abduct and murder me?" She kept her voice perfectly level, but surprise sparked in the court reporter's eyes. She should have warned the poor woman that this was unlikely to be a run-of-the-mill deposition.

"I'm talking about the incident where those gentlemen boarded the ship while we were docked in Thai waters, which—if you would read the Act closely—is not a situation where it governs. We were under the jurisdiction of the Thai authorities and I properly reported that regrettable situation to the Royal Thailand Police, as you know, as well as your embassy, even though I was under no regulatory obligation to do so. I simply thought it was the right thing to do."

Sasha arched a brow at that characterization. "We'll get back to the attempted abduction later, but can we agree that Mr. McGraw and Mr. Williams are both citizens of the United States?"

"I suppose we can agree to that," he said, answering carefully, as though he suspected a trick but couldn't quite tease out what she was up to.

She smiled. "Great. Good. So, it's your position that even though two American nationals boarded your ship with the intent to commit a violent crime against me—a third American national—you were under no obligation to note the incident in your log book or to report it to the authorities because it did not occur at sea. Do I have that right?"

"Yes, exactly." His tone was one of a teacher taking pride that a particularly slow student had finally figured out a difficult concept. She half-expected him to say 'Well done!'

"If they had boarded the ship at a different time, say, for instance, when we were in the Gulf of Thailand in the area that is contested, would you have reported it then?"

"Certainly," he said immediately. He puffed out his chest, "There are several nautical miles that could belong to either the Thai or the Vietnamese or the Malaysians—or even the Cambodians. In that situation, I would have reported it forthwith to the nearest United States Legal Attaché."

"Why?"

"Because the portion of the gulf that is so hotly disputed as to be under no nation's control would, under any reasonable reading, fall under your country's CVSSA. Do you see the difference?" He leaned forward, eager to embarrass her with his superior knowledge.

"I think I do, but let's make sure. If a U.S. citizen committed a violent crime in *that* part of the sea and it was brought to your attention by a passenger, you'd report it, right?"

He licked his lips nervously and patted that right jacket pocket again. "I would if the crime occurred on my ship."

He knew where she was going. So much for walking him into a trap.

"Why do you draw that distinction, Captain?"

He hesitated. "Because you did come to me on the morning of the third day of the cruise, when were in an unclaimed, or contested area in the South China Sea, claiming to have witnessed a crime on a nearby fishing boat."

"What crime did I say I saw, Captain?"

"You know full well."

"For the record, please."

He gave her a sour look, then he seemed to re-member he was being filmed. "You said that you saw two men shoot a woman on another boat."

"Did you note that in your log?"

"No."

"Did you report it to nearest Legat?"

"No, I did not. And from what I've heard, the dead woman was a citizen of Malaysia."

"You heard she was Malaysian?"

"That's right."

"From whom?

He stammered. "I ... don't recall."

She didn't actually care where he'd heard it, but she sat in silence for a moment, letting him stew.

He patted his pocket.

"When did you hear this rumor? Do you recall *that*?" She used an acid tone.

"No, I'm afraid I don't."

"Let's stick to reality. Mr. McGraw and Mr. Wil-liams are American citizens, correct? You haven't heard otherwise from any mystery sources, have you?"

He glared. "No."

"When did you report that incident?"

"I didn't."

She feigned surprise. "You didn't? But you received a report from a passenger on a U.S.-owned cruise ship of an incident involving U.S. nationals who were perpetrating a violent crime in international waters. Isn't that right?"

"Yes."

"The Act requires you to report that, doesn't it?" She smiled.

"I don't ... well, I don't know. The incident didn't occur on my cruise ship." He was visibly rattled now.

"Does the Act say anything about that?"

"I'm ... not sure."

"Let's consider a hypothetical. If a pair of pirates were shooting at your ship in international waters, but they missed, would you report that?"

"Well, yes."

"Why? In that case, the incident wouldn't have occurred on your ship."

"But it would have involved my ship." The statement came out more like a question.

She fired again. "Is it your position that a report of a crime made to you on your ship by a passenger on your ship somehow *doesn't* involve your ship?"

He opened his mouth. "Uh ... no. I mean, I don't ... I'm not sure."

Got him.

Sasha counted silently in her head. *One. Two. And there it was. The pat.*

"Tell you what. We'll come back to this. Let's move on for now, shall we?"

"Yes, let's." Relief flooded his expression.

"Okay, you gave up your command of *The Water Lily* to take over as captain of *The Viola*, correct?"

"Yes. After the harrowing events on my last cruise, I determined that it was time for a change to a new route."

"So you moved from the South China Sea route to a Baltimore to Quebec City round-trip route, right?"

"That's correct."

"Would you consider that to be a demotion?"

"I assuredly would not. Aside from the fact that *The Viola* is a fine ship, an excellent, seaworthy vessel, I voluntarily chose to make the change. Demotions are not voluntary, Mrs. Connelly." He drew himself up and squared his shoulders.

"It's Ms. McCandless-Connelly, actually. Or counselor if that's easier for you to remember. Let's talk about the new route. It's very similar to your former route, right?"

He looked at her as though she were drooling on the table. "In what way would you equate a cruise with stops in Singapore, Bangkok, and Ho

Chi Minh City with a cruise from Baltimore to Canada and back? Lovely as it is, it's a very different route."

"Sure, the weather and the scenery are different. But the heroin's the same, isn't it?"

He froze. "I beg your pardon?"

The court reporter's eyes bugged out.

Sasha breezed along. "Well, your old route was along The Golden Triangle, the sweet spot for heroin distribution from Asia. And your new route is out of Baltimore, one of two terminuses for the United States' very own Heroin Highway. So, from your perspective as a drug smuggler, they're the same, right?"

He half-rose from his seat, noticed the red eye of the camera, and slowly lowered himself back down, patting his jacket pocket as he did so. "Madam, I must warn you—"

She raised a hand and cut him off. "No, Captain. I need to warn you. You are under oath. And you may not know this, but you're not the only one giving testimony under oath. Your friends, Mr. Williams and Mr. McGraw have been offered immunity from prosecution by the Royal Thailand Police in exchange for their testimony against Thale and they've been offered immunity by the government of the United States in exchange for their testimony about ... other matters. I think we both know what those other matters are, Captain."

He shook his head and sputtered, "They're liars. Who would believe them?"

"Oh, Captain, who would take the word of a washed-up junkie over two U.S. military veterans?" Her voice was soft, almost gentle. "This is your chance to get your side of the story out. It's likely your only chance before you're charged with drug smuggling."

He lowered his eyes to the table for a moment then looked up at her. "How did you know?"

She shook her head. "No, that's not how this works. I ask the questions; you answer the questions. Did you buy your heroin from Bar Pavot?"

His face turned a red, mottled color. "I refuse to answer that."

"Did you go along with Thale's plan to let McGraw and Williams climb onto the boat, give them access to my suite, and let them abduct me because they were holding your personal drug use over your head or because you were in too deep in the drug smuggling operation to say no?"

"I refuse to answer."

Sasha paused in her questioning. "In the interest of a clean transcript, you need to say that you're invoking your Fifth Amendment right not to answer on the ground that you might incriminate yourself. Or you can stop the deposition and try to find an attorney to represent you. I can give you the number for the public defender's office if you like."

He folded his arms across his chest and pressed his lips into a thin line. No response.

She continued, "That day on the ship, Derek Williams yelled at you and said if you didn't help them Thale would find another dragon shuttle. Was that a reference to the fact that you were smuggling heroin from Bangkok to Singapore on *The Water Lily?*"

He shook his head wordlessly from side to side.

"Counsel notes for the record that the deponent is shaking his head no but refuses to answer my question. Moving on, how much heroin do you move on *The Viola?*"

He exploded out of his chair. "I have had quite enough of this. This is an outrage."

Sasha smiled. "How many heroin cigarettes do you have in your jacket pocket, Captain?"

He glared at her, with his hands fisted at his sides.

Any day now, Connelly, she thought.

A moment later, Connelly and Hank barreled through the door.

45.

HANK CAME BACK into the conference room holding a silver cigarette case.

"Where's the captain?" Sasha asked. After Hank and Leo had tackled him and given him the *Miranda* warning, Hank had handcuffed him and hustled him out of the room in a hurry.

"I had some DEA guys on standby. Just in case. They met me in front of the building and I handed him off. You know, international drug smuggling is more in line with their mission than ours." He jerked a thumb at Connelly.

Whatever that mission might be, Sasha thought.

"What's with the case?" Connelly asked.

"It's evidence, obviously, but they had a dog with them, so they asked me to hang on to it so Champ didn't go nuts all the way back to the office." He pried the case open and held it up for Sasha and Connelly to see the innocuous-looking heroin cigarettes nestled inside.

"So, to answer your question, he had four," Hank said.

Connelly leaned against the wall and looked at her. "How *did* you know?"

"All the pieces just fit together. The mercenaries did yell at him about a dragon shuttle when they were looking for me. When I started reading up about Baltimore's heroin problem last night, I saw a quote about 'chasing the dragon,' which is slang for smoking heroin. And that got me thinking."

"That's it? A throwaway reference to a dragon shuttle?"

She hesitated. "Well, the other thing was that Mel said Thale's a big drug trafficker. It sounded like the Bureau suspected Thale of using its shipping fleet to move the drugs. But ... all the nightmares you have about being on that boat, you always talk about the conditions and the men. You never mentioned drugs. And Vũ's cooperating but he didn't try to use information about heroin smuggling as a bargaining chip to lessen his charges. Don't you think he would have?"

Hank shrugged. "Probably. Guys usually try to deal with everything they've got. There's no reason why he'd hold information back if he had it."

"So, it didn't seem like Thale was using its own fleet, which would be really risky anyway. But they had to be moving the drugs somehow. It just made sense. Especially when van Metier transferred to a Baltimore route—he knew he was going to lose a lucrative side job and possibly end up implicated in the case against Thale. It was time to move on."

All the facts had gelled into place. Yes, she'd broken the cardinal rule of depositions and asked a question she didn't know the answer to. But she figured if it had all gone to hell on her, she could always wrap up with the question about the heroin cigarettes in his pocket. She *knew* she was right about that part. He'd been so squirrelly about touching his pocket. It was such a giveaway.

"You're something else. You know that?" Connelly dipped his head down and spoke close to her ear. "Have I really been talking in my sleep?"

She cut her eyes over to Hank and then nodded. "Yes."

He held her gaze for a long moment.

Then the court reporter, who'd been busily packing up all her equipment walked over. Sasha broke eye contact with her husband, but this subject wasn't closed.

"I assume you want an expedited file?" The court reporter asked, all business—as if what had just happened was a regular occurrence.

"Yes, please. I'll take the rough as soon as you can get it to me."

The woman nodded. "The camera was running when these two came in and took your deponent into custody. Do you want me to edit it out?"

Sasha thought for a moment then shook her head no. "Leave it in."

"Will do." She shouldered her carrying cases and Hank held the door for her. As she was on her way out, he said, "So tell me, are all depositions that dang boring?"

The court reporter's jaw fell open. "Are you serious? That was the most exciting deposition I've witnessed in twenty-seven years in this business."

Connelly and Hank groaned in unison.

"It was hard to stay awake watching that," Connelly confessed.

"Boy, am I glad I never went to law school," Hank said with a fake shudder.

The videographer looked at Sasha and shook her head. "If they only knew."

46.

LEO GRINNED AT Sasha over the top of Finn's head. It was the perfect summer day. The weather wasn't oppressively hot, and a light breeze played on the air. It was a great day for an afternoon ballgame—even if he'd had to drag her out of the office past a bevy of reporters looking for a quote about 'Captain Heroin.' After van Metier's arrest, the Drug Enforcement Administration had sent teams through *The Water Lily* and *The Viola* to comb through storage compartments. According to Hank, they'd found enough trace heroin on *The Water Lily* to justify charges in both Thailand and Singapore. A cross-border team was hammering out the details. He put van Metier out of his mind and focused on their family day at the ballpark.

At some point, without his quite noticing, enthusiasm for the sports teams of his adopted hometown had seeped into his bones and established itself. Leo was fairly certain he was a more ardent Steelers and Penguins fan than was his Pittsburgh-born and -bred wife. That said, he couldn't quite touch her passion for the Pirates. She'd been born within a month of the Pirates 1979 World Series win and seemed to feel a special connection to the team—despite, or maybe because of, the fact that the club hadn't appeared in a single World Series since.

She smiled back at him. "What are you thinking?" she asked, keeping one eye on Fiona, who had clambered up onto the granite base of the bigger than life-sized Roberto Clemente statue and was now attempting to scale the sports legend's leg.

Their daughter was apparently undaunted by the fact that the leg in question was slick bronze or that she was not exactly sturdy on her feet. Finn watched her try to pull herself up; his expression was a mixture of admiration and worry. It was a familiar mix of emotions to Leo—he often felt it with regard to Sasha.

"I'm thinking about him," he said in answer to Sasha's question. He nodded toward Roberto Clemente.

"Really?"

"He never stopped trying to help people. He never forgot where he came from—he used his talents and his money to give back." He tried to keep his tone lighthearted.

But she narrowed her eyes and considered him for a long time. He could tell she was thinking about his father, but before he could tell her she was wrong, Fiona managed to make it to Clemente's knee.

"Connelly—"

"Fiona!" He pointed, and Sasha turned to see their eleven-month old pulling herself to the statue's thigh.

They both thrust their hands out underneath her in case she toppled backward. Finn started babbling his name for her in a high-pitched baby squeal. "Fee, Fee!"

Inexplicably, she managed to cling to the metal like a baby monkey. She gave each of her parents a look that showed great displeasure at their lack of faith in her. She cooed back at her brother. Sasha shook her head.

"She's your daughter," Leo informed her.

Finn picked this moment remind them that he had a few tricks of his own. He toddled off after a pigeon, leaning forward and leading with his top-heavy baby noggin. Leo strode after him and scooped him up under one arm, lessening the indignity with a barrage of tickles.

Over Finn's squeals of delight, he said, "We should get moving; the game's about to start."

Sasha pried Fiona off the statue and the family started across the bridge to the ballpark, each adult holding tight to a chubby little hand.

~ ~ ~ ~ ~ ~ ~ ~ ~ ~

It was the bottom of the sixth with runners on second and third. The twins, having exhausted themselves by climbing up and down the ramps for an inning and a half, had both dozed off. Sasha was trying to decide whether she should risk disturbing Finn, who was asleep on her lap, by flagging down a concession worker for a lemonade or maybe a beer.

Beside her, Connelly kept his eyes pinned on the batter and said, "I need to ask you for a favor."

'Favor' struck her as an odd choice of words. She glanced over at him, but he was still staring straight ahead.

"Ask away."

After a pause, he said, "I want to use the vacation house fund for something else."

She waited, but he didn't appear to be planning to elaborate.

"The vacation house fund?" she echoed even though she was certain she'd heard him correctly.

"Yes."

The crack of the bat interrupted their conversation. They cheered as the runner crossed the plate.

Connelly reached around Fiona to record the play. He was just like her dad. A large part of his enjoyment of the game came from keeping score. She waited until he finished making the notation.

"Do you mind telling me what you'd like to spend the money on?"

"Does it matter?"

"Well, yes, actually, it does. If you want to set a mistress up with a place of her own, the answer's no. If you want to go back to school and get an art history degree or something, the answer is yes."

He chuckled. "An art degree? Really?"

She shrugged. "It was the best I could come up with. Seriously, Connelly, what's going on?"

"I can't stop thinking about Binh. And the others. I want to use the money to help them."

She considered mentioning that helping the sea slaves would also enable him to change his family's legacy. Duc Nguyen was a murderer and a thief. His son could choose a different path. But she knew better than to bring up his father.

Instead, she said, "You did help them. Vũ's in prison. Thale is under indictment." She put a hand on his arm. "Nobody's sleeping in cages anymore. Binh's happy in Phu My. And Thiha Bo's doing great, working in the fish market and going to university."

He shook his head. "Only because I wandered onto that boat. Can you even imagine how many Binhs and Thiha Bos—and Minas—are still out on the ocean, trawling for cheap fish to make cat food?"

She couldn't imagine. Or, to be honest, she didn't want to. She knew there must be hundreds, maybe thousands of them. And although she hadn't mentioned it to him since the day at the deposition, she also knew he was still having nightmares about the boat. She heard him saying the names, speaking in Vietnamese, tortured in his dreams by the memory of what he'd seen.

She took a deep breath. "I guess it's like Roberto Clemente said—Any time you have an opportunity to make a difference in this world and you don't, you're wasting your time on Earth. It's something like that, at any rate—I might be paraphrasing."

Connelly turned and gaped at her.

"You're going to miss the play," she said.

He kept staring. Finally he said, "Is that a yes?"

"It's not a no." Finn stirred against her chest, and she smoothed his wavy, baby chick tuff of hair. "It's a yes with strings."

Connelly's gray eyes narrowed. "What kind of strings?"

"You have two small children and a wife who really doesn't want to have to learn how to cook like some sort of adult. You also kind of have a job. You can't go traipsing off to Southeast Asia to buy out indentured servants' contracts all the time. Plus, that doesn't really help the fishermen. Yes, it gets them out of their immediate crisis. But it's not sustained—or sustainable. I mean, we *will* eventually run out of money. You need to be smart about how you do this."

"So what do you suggest?"

She chewed on her lower lip while she thought. "Call the Kurcks."

He blinked. "Elli and Oliver?"

"Sure. She's a professor of social justice. He's an investment banker. Between the three of you, you should be able to come up with a plan to fund a multi-pronged program to work with the existing seafarer support centers over there. You really need to address the systemic issues that are driving people onto those boats in the first place."

"You're brilliant."

"I know."

"And modest, too." He leaned over and kissed her hard on the lips, careful to cradle Fiona's head so she wouldn't collide into Finn's noggin.

She kissed him back harder. Then she smiled and leaned against his shoulder. Just then they watched the Pirates' hottest slugger smash the ball. It sailed over the right field wall. The park erupted. Over the cheers, she said, "You know that wall's twenty-one feet high?"

"Is that so?"

"Yep. In honor of Clemente. He wore number 21."

"You're just a fount of knowledge, aren't you?"

"I try, Connelly. I really try."

Author's Note

As always, I hope you enjoyed reading this book. Every book I write changes me in some way—sometimes it's a small thing; sometimes it's a large thing. This book changed me in a big way. All the books in the Sasha McCandless series involve plots that *could* happen. *International Incident* involves a plot that *is happening*, and that affected me.

I set this book on an international cruise mainly so that I didn't have to write umpteen scenes involving infant twins. (It's true.) When I started to think about the possible crimes and legal issues that could arise on an international cruise, I hit on human trafficking and drug trafficking. Then I started to research in earnest, and what I learned about human trafficking and modern slavery was so dark and unpleasant that I put this book aside for awhile. If you're interested in reading more (nonfiction) about the issue of sea slavery and conditions on fishing boats, a good starting point is a multi-part series of articles published by *The New York Times* in 2015 called "The Outlaw Ocean" and a July 2015 article published by *The Guardian*.

The investigative pieces published by these two entities shined a light on the issue (and prompted the United States government to enact legislation to close a legal loophole earlier this year.) Even as I worked on other projects, I kept thinking about the sea slaves I'd read about. And I knew I had to write this book.

But I also knew I couldn't *just* write this book. I had to, in the words of the late, great Roberto Clemente, also do something. So this is what I'm doing:

I'm making educated choices about the brands and products that I buy (including my own Java's cat food as well as the products that feed my coffee and dark chocolate habits) and supporting rescue and advocacy efforts. The following websites provide a good starting point to learn about the larger issue of slave labor

and how to take action: End Slavery Now
and Free the Slaves; and

I'm also supporting Human Rights
at Sea, a registered charitable organization
in the United Kingdom that works "to
explicitly raise awareness, implementation
and accountability of human rights
provisions throughout the maritime
environment, especially where they are
currently absent, ignored or being abused"
and The International Seafarers' Welfare
and Assistance Network (ISWAN)

ABOUT THE AUTHOR

USA Today bestselling author Melissa F. Miller was born in Pittsburgh, Pennsylvania. Although life and love led her to Philadelphia, Baltimore, Washington, D.C., and, ultimately, South Central Pennsylvania, she secretly still considers Pittsburgh home.

In college, she majored in English literature with concentrations in creative writing poetry and medieval literature and was STUNNED, upon graduation, to learn that there's not exactly a job market for such a degree. After working as an editor for several years, she returned to school to earn a law degree. She was that annoying girl who loved class and always raised her hand. She practiced law for fifteen years, including a stint as a clerk for a federal judge, nearly a decade as an attorney at major international law firms, and several years running a two-person law firm with her lawyer husband.

Now, powered by coffee, she writes legal thrillers and homeschools her three children. When she's not writing, and sometimes when she is, Melissa travels around the country in an RV with her husband, her kids, and her cat.

Thank You!

Sasha and Leo will back in their next adventure soon; stay tuned for details! In the meantime, please feel free to check out my other books.

If you enjoy this series, I'd love if you would help others enjoy it, too.

Share it. This book is lending-enabled; so please lend your copy to a friend who might like it.

Review it. Please consider posting a short review to help other readers decide whether they might enjoy it.

Connect with me. Stop by my Facebook page for book updates, cover reveals, quotes about coffee, and general time-wasting at https://www.facebook.com/authormelissafmiller.

CPSIA information can be obtained
at www.ICGtesting.com
Printed in the USA
BVHW04s1959091018
529709BV00012B/770/P

9 781940 759197